# AMERICAN PENNY

To:
Jo Ann and Tom
Best Wishes,
Good Neighbors,
Patricia Bowen Pope

# AN
# AMERICAN
# PENNY

*A young girl's most amazing and unexpected adventure*

## PATRICIA BOWEN POPE

YorkshirePublishing
www.yorkshirepublishing.com
*Write Now.*

ISBN: 978-1-946977-75-5
*An American Penny*
Copyright © 2016 by Patricia Bowen Pope

For permission requests, write to the publisher at the address below.

Yorkshire Publishing
3207 South Norwood Avenue
Tulsa, Oklahoma 74135
www.YorkshirePublishing.com
918.394.2665

# Acknowledgments

For my dear family and friends who encouraged me to write this story, my husband, Dwight, and editor, Jacqueline Nelson, Adjunct Professor of English at the Johnson County Community College, thank you for your time, judgment, and insights.

This is a story of families faced with difficult decisions regarding their children's welfare and the family members and friends who come to their rescue. It is a fictional story inspired by true events as seen through the eyes of a child. The time frame is shortly following World War II. It describes sacrifice and love freely given without thought of reciprocity.

# Contents

# 1

# Something Must Be Done

We were finally home. The family had been looking for my baby sister for hours. Mother had even asked some of the neighbors to help search the area in which Elizabeth Ann was last seen. She would be four years old in a few months, in June. Ann, as we called her, was a bright little girl who was very curious and walked early or, maybe I should say, ran early! She had been playing outside in the front of the house and wandered off before we knew it—and not for the first time!

Just before supper that night, we found her in our neighbor's automobile fast asleep. This neighbor's daughter had a habit of leaving the back door of their car not quite shut. Curious Ann had gone down the street, climbed into the backseat, and fallen asleep. When my father came home from work early that evening, he was very angry.

"This is not good," he said. "Something must be done!"

We had heard him say this before about other issues. It often meant that some changes to our family situation would soon occur. For example, on occasion, Father would remind all of us to look out for the younger ones. That meant Margaret and I should check on the younger ones more often. But this time, he seemed very angry by Ann's disappearance. We didn't know what changes to our family situation he might affect this time after such a declaration.

The first time I had heard my father exclaim that something must be done had been before Ann was born. That was about four years ago right after World War II ended. In 1945, school had just begun when we had heard the war was over. Everyone was talking about it. News about the victory covered the front page of the newspapers and was constantly being discussed on the radio. The reporters spoke very quickly and were acting excited. I was glad but didn't quite know why except everyone I met was smiling or laughing.

As for Mother and Father, I never knew for sure what the war being over really meant for them. I knew my mother didn't have to use ration stamps anymore, and Father had said he was glad he could buy new tires instead of getting them repaired. He would say, "They have so many patches on them now. I don't have any place left to patch!" Even though Father wasn't usually very picky about his food and day-to-day things, he loved his morning coffee. He didn't like it when Mother would limit the amount he could have at one time. She would say, "Remember why we are using stamps and why they are limited. The boys overseas need their rations more than we do." He would shrug his shoulders and change the subject. He wouldn't ask for another cup, at least for a few days. I think he knew Mother was right. The end of the war meant the end of such tight rationing.

I was glad the war was over. Some things seemed to be getting better and easier except that Mother was resting and in bed more than usual. Father always looked like he was thinking about other things when I talked to him, but all the other people I knew were smiling more and didn't seem as sad or as serious as my parents. Of course, I didn't really know that many other people. Most of the people I did know were usually friends of my parents, or they were neighbors or friends at school or church.

My name is Penelope, but my family and friends call me Penny. I was six years old and in kindergarten at Woodrow Wilson School right after the war ended. I'm what was called a middle child, actually one of three middle children, and lived with my mother and father, big sister, little sister, and two little brothers. We lived in what you would call a medium-sized four-bedroom house. We had three floors, an attic, a basement, and a garage that sits next to our alley. Father often tells us our city, Kansas City, keeps growing, just like our family.

I heard people say we lived in America's "breadbasket" because of the farms we had around us that grew wheat and for the many stockyards and for the cattle the farmers on nearby farms had. I had never been on a farm, but my mother and father liked to take rides in the country on Sundays after church. We would see lots of farms. I used to imagine that I would have liked living on some of the farms, especially those with fields of wheat that seemed to be waving at us when we drove by and the wind was blowing. Some farms had cattle and ponds with lots of land and trees to play on.

Although my sisters and brothers didn't like going for rides in the country, I really did. However, there were so many places to go to and see in the city. We had nice neighbors and friends living in the city, which was good too. Besides, this city is where my family lived, so as long as I was with my family, I felt happy.

One family of friends we enjoyed lived down the street from us on the corner. The Abernathys had two daughters who lived with them and a son. I think their son was lost or hurt because he didn't come home when the war was over. They told my mother they "lost him in the war and that he was missing in action." I thought he may have died or was hurt and didn't remember where he lived, but I never wanted to say anything about what I thought.

They didn't ask my opinion; I was just listening when they said this as they were having coffee one day with my parents at our house. They weren't the only family we knew that had missing members due to the war. We knew more in our church. One of my friends in school said her uncle didn't come home. Our pastor held special services for the families with missing members. My parents went to many of the services, but I didn't go.

A new friend to our family was a lady that lived in our house on the third floor, Mrs. Kessler. Since she needed a place to live and was helping my mother, she moved into the house after Father made an apartment on the third floor. It was really the attic, but Mother and Father made it into an apartment. Mother was very busy taking care of us. Since she was going to have a new baby in the summer, Father told us Mother needed some help with household duties and that was why Mrs. Kessler came to live with us.

Mrs. Kessler was a tall, big woman, bigger than my dad. When I first met her, I was a little afraid of her. But she was friendly, and she would cook delicious and different food for us that I had never tasted before. She made potato pancakes and large meat dishes "to fill us up," she'd say. Mrs. Kessler also made lots of desserts and would let us watch her for a while as she cooked, if we were quiet.

Another one of our friends and neighbors lived behind us in a very tall white house with three flights of stairs on the back. They were the Lugenbiehls. They were all pale-looking with blond hair like me, but they were also very tall. Their daughter, Glenda, played with my older sister, Margaret.

We sometimes called Margaret "Peggy" except when Mother and Father wanted her in a hurry. Sometimes Margaret and Glenda would let me play with them, even though I was only six years old. I loved being with them because they were fun and laughed a lot.

I wouldn't talk much, but that was because I didn't know what to say. Sometimes I would just listen, which was much more interesting to me. Sometimes when I didn't know what they were talking about, I would ask questions. Instead of answering my questions, they would tell me to go home, so I learned to be quiet and stop asking questions if I wanted to stay and play with them.

Of course, much of our time was also spent in school. I was in kindergarten at the Woodrow Wilson School, which was only a few blocks up the hill from my house. I loved school and liked knowing everyone in my class. I would walk to and from school every day. The part of the walk home that I dreaded was going past the house where the mean dog lived on the hill going down to our street. I prayed every day he would be asleep and not chase me when I passed his yard.

One day when I was walking home from school, the dog was barking more than usual and broke away from his porch, chasing me down the hill. I was running as fast as I could and ran into the street without looking in front of me. I didn't see the car coming. It screeched to a stop. I thought it touched me. I didn't feel any pain or anything but was very scared and began to cry.

My mother, who always had strong ears, said she heard me scream and then the car screeching. A neighbor and Mrs. Kessler, who came running out, carried me into the house and placed me in bed while Mother watched. The doctor came to our house to see me and said, "She doesn't have any bruises, and it doesn't look like the car hit her, but she should be watched for a couple of days. Call if you have questions."

I knew I wasn't really hurt. I wanted to play games with Margaret and listen to the radio programs that evening with my family. Since there was no school the next day, my parents let me lie on the couch instead so I could listen to the radio. *Hopalong Cassidy*, *Fibber McGee and Molly*, and *The Lone Ranger* were three of my favorites.

My father was very angry about my car accident. He stood in front of us with his hands on his hips as he said, "The car was going too fast, and it was too much for Mother to watch over all of you. Something must be done!"

The first consequence of my father's declaration was that he and Mother talked to Mrs. Kessler. The second consequence was when he said, "For now, Mrs. Kessler will spend more time taking care of you because of our expected baby and because your mother will need more rest."

I was very worried about Mother. She had dark circles below her eyes and often disappeared into her room a lot, shutting her door. Father asked us to play quietly and to not make so much noise. That was hard for us because there were so many of us. We tried to play more board games and made tunnels in the basement or played in the backyard until it got too cold.

Mother's tummy was getting bigger. She told us the new baby would be coming in June. It was a good thing Mrs. Kessler was helping her because one day, Mother was just too tired to get out of bed. The doctor came to see her that evening, so we all went to bed early.

A few days later, my father had some important news to tell us, but he said it would have to wait until after dinner. I was so worried I could hardly eat my dinner. Mostly, I was afraid it was about mother and his announcement after my accident that something must be done.

After dinner, my father asked us to stay at the dining room table. He said he had something to tell us. He was very cheerful, smiling, and laughing. I think he was trying to make us all feel better and to not worry.

He told us, "Mother will need to be in bed for a few months until the baby is born to keep her and the baby safe. It would be better if Margaret, Penny, and Henry would be taken care of by Aunt Martha and her husband, Harold, in Canada." Father added that Katherine and Albert were too young to be separated from their mother and father and that the distance was too far for them to go.

I had only met Aunt Martha and Uncle Harold once, so I didn't really know them. They lived in Canada where my uncle was a dentist in a small town named Hillbrook.

Martha and Harold had been married for some years. They didn't have any children and apparently wanted us to come live with them to finish the school year there and until the baby came. They had a big house and could take care of us. Martha was older than my dad, and she was his only sister.

Margaret started to cry and said she wasn't going to Martha and Harold's. My little brother, Henry, who was too young for school didn't do anything, but I felt sort of sick to my stomach. My mother looked very sad and tried to help us by saying it would be very nice staying with them and that we would like it there. She added that we would only be there a short time and that it would be like we were going on vacation. "Canada has Eskimos, igloos, and things we had seen in pictures in books," she said.

You're not to worry because Uncle Harold and Aunt Martha love you and want to have you come for a visit. You can go to school there to finish out the year and come home shortly after the new baby is born."

I asked where Canada was and how we would get there. My father told us that Canada was in the north and that Aunt Martha would come to Kansas City for a visit and take us back to her home in Canada by train.

That evening, Margaret, who was thirteen years old, told me that Eskimos kissed by rubbing their noses together and that she wasn't going to Canada. Nonetheless, Mother took us out of school the next day and got our records transferred to the school in Hillbrook. So for a few days, I tried to forget about going away and played with my sister and brothers as much as I could. Margaret stayed mostly in her room.

# 2

# Setting Out

A few weeks later, Aunt Martha came for her visit. She said Uncle Harold had to work and couldn't come along, as he was the only dentist in Hillbrook and had patients to care for. Aunt Martha had brown hair, was bigger than my mother, but was very nice and quiet. I liked her. She helped Mother get us all ready to go.

My sister kept saying she wasn't going, but Mother told her she would have to go to help Aunt Martha with my brother, Henry, and me. I felt sorry for Margaret. She didn't want to leave her friends, and she didn't like to go to unfamiliar places. But then for a few days, we were very busy getting ready and packing our things.

When the day to leave arrived, we all said good-bye, hugged, and kissed Mother as well as our brother and sister. Mother had tears in her eyes. Margaret was crying as we climbed into Father's Chevrolet with Aunt Martha to go to the train station.

We were catching the train at Union Station. It was a huge building with shiny floors and high ceilings. Father told us there were many trains here in the station. The building had many train tracks that went to other cities in America as well as Canada. There were many people there to catch their train with their suitcases and packages. The inside of the building had high ceilings that had beautiful paintings on them. The ceiling looked higher to me than the art gallery ceilings in our city.

Mother had taken Margaret and me to the art gallery on Saturday mornings to see children's movies and for other events. The art gallery was another beautiful large building. It was surrounded by green lawns. I remembered visiting and how I felt very small there, especially when Margaret or Mother was out of my sight. I was a little worried I might get lost, surrounded by the beautiful paintings and the art I was looking at. Some of the paintings were so beautiful I would look at them and lose sight of Mother or Margaret. Mother told me there were ladies in the rooms to help you if you thought you were lost. I never had to ask for help.

Union Station didn't have paintings and art. It was the biggest and busiest place I had ever seen. We could hear the whistles from the trains and the hissing and grinding of the engines as they came and went. Loud announcements of the next train arriving or departing were sounded over the loud speakers. All around us, people were bustling and rushing in and out of the station, carrying their suitcases and packages and saying hello and good-bye to their families.

Before we boarded our train, all of us went to the restroom except Aunt Martha. She said she would wait outside the door to the restrooms and listen for our call to board the train. Margaret took Henry's hand, and we all went into the restroom.

When I was washing my hands, a young woman was also there combing her hair. She had dark brown hair and a nice face. She looked about the age of my teacher at Woodrow Wilson School. I noticed the pretty ring she was wearing and told her how much I liked it.

It was very different from any I had ever seen. It had a woman's face carved on the front in white with a dark background. She thanked me and said it was very special to her. I asked her where she was going. She told me she had just arrived after a very long journey and wasn't going anywhere else. She said she was very happy to be here.

She asked me, "Do you live here, and do you like it? Are you going on a trip?"

I told her, "Yes, we are going to visit Canada."

She was smiling and said as she was leaving, "I hope you have a nice journey."

"Thank you," I said, and then we hurried out of the bathroom. My sister told me I shouldn't talk to strangers.

In the lobby of the station, I saw the same lady walk up to an older man, and they spoke to each other for a few minutes. They shook hands, and then she pulled a notebook out of her coat pocket, looked at it for a minute, hugged the man, and began walking out of the station.

The man she had spoken to then went to the ticket line and was soon in line with us as we were walking up to the train going to Canada.

# 3

# Lauren

Lauren was so relieved she was almost "home." It had taken her so long to get here, and the future looked hopeful. Thank God the war was over, and she had been able to get a visa. It had been such a long and difficult trip. At first, she had flown to England from France and then to Canada, and now she was in America and ready to start a new life.

Thoughts raced through her mind as fast and wildly as the people who swirled and jostled around her in the station. What would her aunt, her mother's sister, and her uncle think of her?

Lauren was only a young student when they immigrated to America. Did they have enough money to support her for a while until she could get on her feet? she wondered. What kind of work would she be able to get? The soldiers coming back home would need jobs, but she would take any job that she could find.

She thought perhaps she might be able to work as an assistant in a university or a business because of her education at the convent and training at the engineering company in Paris. She had done well academically at the convent. Maybe she could teach French, she thought.

Getting her certifications from France would be difficult, though, and may take a long time, but surely it would not be impossible. It occurred to her that she may have to go back to school and receive additional education to work in the United States.

Lauren had been devastated when her mother, a teacher, had disappeared from the school in which she taught. When her mother failed to return home after the school day was closed, she inquired at the school and was told Nazi soldiers had taken her from the school for questioning. Her father, who had joined the resistance earlier, had also disappeared. She feared the worst and turned to her parents' oldest friends, Louie and Marie, for support. She knew they could be trusted.

They advised Lauren to leave her apartment and move in with them. They owned a bakery that had a small extra room that she could use. They suggested she should continue her current job for a very short time and then tell her employer she would be leaving Paris for another job. In addition, she should be very discrete with her other friends and maintain her privacy, not knowing who could be trustworthy. Unfortunately, unwittingly, they might say something to the wrong parties.

Louie and Marie said they would tell their friends that Lauren was a niece who needed a job and was from another city in France. She could help in the bakery. She would also tell the couple who managed her parents' apartment building she would be leaving Paris for another job.

Lauren quickly began implementing her plans. She moved in with her parents' friends, the Louises. She gave notice at her workplace, told a few friends she was leaving Paris, and started a new life.

She moved into the bakery and her small room. She began to help at the bakery, working evenings and early morning hours. When she wasn't working to help Louie and Marie, she spent her time upstairs with them in their apartment. She learned to stay out of the eyes of the bakery customers during the day hours of business to limit her exposure.

She became very fond of Louie and Marie and spent many hours in their apartment, sharing meals and just talking. They became the only friends she had. Louie and Marie went to church every day and would come back to the bakery with any news they had learned to share with her. The days turned into months and the months into years.

Then the war was over, and the allies were actively assisting in the recovery. Lauren began to feel hope for the first time in years. She thought about her younger sister, whom she knew not where, and her aunt and uncle, who hopefully were in the United States. Then she thought about Louie and Marie. What will they do? She would talk to them, and when she did, they encouraged her to think ahead and "make her own choices." They were the best friends anyone could want.

She decided to go to the United States to look for her aunt and uncle. They were the last remaining members of her family she had hopes of finding. *If Lisa is in Ireland with Kathleen, maybe they can help me find her*, she thought.

She hurried out of the train station depot and began looking for the cab Mr. Cowan said would be waiting for her. She looked up and was immediately struck by the intact skyline of the city, remembering the rubble and destruction she had left behind. She said a prayer. Just then, she saw a cab coming toward her and then stopping.

Faces, familiar faces, were looking at her from the backseat. The cab driver jumped out, opened the door to the backseat for her, and took her bags. Lauren's aunt and uncle both started to talk with her.

Her aunt, who was crying as she got into the cab, said, "Lauren, you're here! We've prayed for this day, and you are here. Let's get you home. You must be very tired."

Lauren smiled at them with such joyfulness. *How long has it been since I've felt tears of joy in my eyes?* she thought. She looked out the window, and calmness came over her. *This is the new world*, she thought. *Thank you, Lord, I'm in America.*

# 4

# Going to Canada

When we got on the train, the ticket collector took our tickets and led us to our seats. The seats were in a separate compartment and were very comfortable. We had brought lunches and ate them. Then we began to feel tired and started to get comfortable except for Aunt Martha. We all napped until she woke us to go to dinner.

As we walked to our table in the dining car, I saw the same older man who had said good-bye to the young lady I had met in the restroom of the train station in Kansas City. He was eating dinner alone. I wondered if he was going to Canada.

After dinner, and in the evening, we read our books and looked out of the windows of the train. It was beginning to get dark outside. The rhythmic noises and movement of the train made me think of home and feel lonely for Mother and Father.

When it became dark outside, we changed for bed and climbed into our train bunks for the night. Margaret and I slept together, while Martha slept with Henry. The hum of the train helped me to fall asleep. Memory of home was then only in my dreams.

I didn't know how many days we were on the train since the train stopped many times to pick up more people and let others off at the many strange and varied towns along the way. I didn't see the older man from the train station again. My home in Kansas City began to feel very far away.

The days on the train felt like one long day after another. Aunt Martha looked happy when we finally arrived at the last town before we were to see Uncle Harold. We were to stop here while the train would change tracks. Soon we would be getting closer to where Uncle Harold was to pick us up in his automobile. We were excited when the train came slowly to a screeching stop.

We were now in Canada. and Uncle Harold was to be here. He was probably waiting for us at the train depot. We began to collect our things to leave the train when just then Aunt Martha saw him.

Uncle Harold called out, almost shouting. He seemed very glad to see Martha and us. He gave us all a big hug. Uncle Harold was tall and thin, had gray hair, and wore glasses. He looked older than my father. He smiled and talked to us as he drove us to a hotel nearby in town where we would stay. He said it would take too long to get home and that we would stay here overnight. "I don't like to drive at night," he said.

The hotel was immense and had a grand staircase in the entryway. The man behind the counter called Uncle Harold by his name when he welcomed us to the hotel. We went to our rooms near an elevator. A man went with us to assist with our suitcases. Our rooms were adjoining. After we washed our hands and combed our hair, we went down the elevator to the hotel dining room where we had dinner.

I had been in an elevator before when Mother had taken us downtown in Kansas City to large stores to shop for school clothes and shoes. When we were downtown, we always ate at the Italian Gardens where ladies behind the glass cases helped us by handing the dishes to us; we then would put them on our trays.

Eating in the hotel dining room was new for me because we had never eaten in a hotel before. The dinner was delicious. We ate chicken and mashed potatoes and pie for dessert. Then we went back to our rooms to sleep.

I couldn't sleep. I was too anxious and excited, wondering what Aunt Martha and Uncle Harold's home would be like. I missed my mother and father very much.

The next morning, we sat down to breakfast in the dining room again. There were a lot of choices on the menu. Uncle Harold ordered oatmeal and fruit for all of us. He informed us that we were not very far from their home and that we were in the town Saskatoon in the province of Saskatchewan in the country of Canada.

When I asked Uncle Harold if a province was like a state in the United States, he said, "Yes, there is a famous town named Lloydminster that is in two provinces, Alberta and Saskatchewan. There aren't many towns in Canada that are in two provinces. In the beginning, when the town started, the people lived in both border provinces. Border provinces are those that are next to each other. Just like your towns of Kansas City, Missouri and Kansas City, Kansas, which are two cities in two states next to each other."

He went on to say, "Lloydminster was founded by the Barr Colonists. They were people who came directly from the country of Great Britain. The town was named for George Lloyd, an Anglican bishop of Saskatchewan." He handed some literature on Lloydminster to Margaret to read to me. He didn't know that I could already read.

Mother had taught me to read. Before she married Father, she had been a teacher's assistant in the very small farming area she was raised in. It was a country school. My mother was very young with only some supervised teacher training. After she graduated with honors from high school, she was offered a position as an assistant at an area school.

I remembered her telling me about her school. Her students were all in the same classroom. She was the teacher for all of them when the supervisor teacher was not in the classroom. The supervisor teacher would develop the teaching plan for the students, and she and Mother would assist the students with the plan.

The supervisor had other schools to supervise, so she was unable to be present in Mother's classroom all day every day. Mother told us when the students were all able to attend school, she might have fifteen students and all the grades through the eighth grade. She told my sister some of the students were taller than her and didn't attend school regularly, especially if they were needed on the family farm to work. Some of them didn't attend school after the sixth grade.

It was during the Depression, and this was the only school for these students at that time. Mother said there was very little extra money for supplies and that she would sometimes buy them with her own money for all to share. Mostly she would buy extra pencils and Big Chief tablets to write on.

She would tell her students, "If you don't have time to learn anything else, you will be glad you learned to read. Read whatever you have—newspapers, magazines, instruction books, and the Bible. Keep reading."

Also, she would say, "Learn your arithmetic. When you can add, subtract, divide, and multiply, you can keep better records and make better choices of what you own and what you sell or buy." I thought this was very good advice for farmers or housewives.

Then I thought of Mr. Thompson who owns the grocery store and Mr. Garrett who works at the drugstore and gives us our medicine. They must be good readers and know how to do arithmetic. I was glad I could read and do most of my multiplication tables. If I practice my arithmetic, I thought it will get easier.

When Mother married Father, he didn't want her to work outside the home, so she stopped teaching. She purchased some children's encyclopedias from a traveling book salesman. Later she would buy books wherever they were sold, and so we had a large number of books at home to read from.

Mother taught Margaret first and then me and Henry. I was very lucky my mother liked to read and that my sister and I caught this enthusiasm for books from her. Henry was beginning to read on his own. He was only four years old.

Aunt Martha interrupted my thoughts. "Have you finished your breakfast, Penny? It's time to set out for home. Are you ready?"

We gathered our things and climbed into Uncle Harold's car as he set off for Hillbrook, their town. We drove, had lunch, and drove some more. Uncle Harold said it would take about five hours to reach their town. We began to get sleepy, especially my little brother, Henry.

I knew Margaret didn't want to come to Canada, but so far the people were friendly and helpful and seemed the same as United States people. Margaret was older than I was and knew a lot more about people and the world.

Even though she was not as friendly with strangers as I was, she was smart and had good ideas. I was very glad she was with me.

Finally, we arrived in Hillbrook. It was a very small town with some stores, churches, and a school building Margaret and I would go to. Martha and Harold's house was brown, tall, and had round turrets, Aunt Martha's word when I asked what they were called. The turrets were shaped like a tower and were on their roof.

They also had a large porch on the front of their house with a swing on it and a garage for their car. There was a large garden in the back of the house. The garden was bare because they had picked all of the vegetables. Aunt Martha said that some of the vegetables were in the cellar and that the weather was too cold to grow anything now. She said, "Everyone had vegetable gardens here during the war, but this next year besides the vegetables, we will plant flowers."

After unloading our things, Aunt Martha showed us to our rooms. Margaret and I were to share a room. It was very pretty with a soft white puffy bedspread and frilly white crisscross curtains on the windows. It had a bedside table with a lamp and dish on it. The dish was colorful with pink, blue, and yellow colors. It was small, but there was room to hold things. There was a nicely sized dresser with drawers for Margaret and me to put our things. Aunt Martha said her company always stayed in our room.

Henry would have a small room next to ours. His room was not as fancy as ours with a plaid bedspread and plain draperies. It had pictures on the wall of boats and a picture of King George. But since Henry had a bookshelf for his toys and books from home, he probably liked it. He spent a lot of time there. Later whenever Aunt Martha was looking for him, we would usually find him there playing with his cars from home or reading.

The rest of the house was full of rooms for different purposes. In the back of the house were the rooms in which Uncle Harold did his dental work. One small room had a desk, chairs, and a small bed. Another room had his dental chair and what looked like tools. Aunt Martha later told me they were not called tools. She called them instruments. I told her that I thought instruments were things like a piano, and she told me with a clipped voice, "Uncle Harold calls them instruments."

I asked Harold about what Aunt Martha had told me, and he said that they are tools but are also called instruments. He also said that when I was around Aunt Martha, I should call them instruments. I said I would. That was when I discovered that two people can both be right and that the best way to get along with Aunt Martha and Uncle Harold was to agree with both of them.

# 5

# Life in Hillbrook

The following week, school enrollment came soon enough. It was fun going to a school that was different from Woodrow Wilson. The days went by quickly. I was glad to meet my new classmates. They were very friendly and wanted to know about my school at home and what it was like living in America.

They asked me if I went to the movies and which actors I liked best. I told them I went to the art gallery on Saturday mornings and saw Walt Disney movies, but I didn't go to other movie theaters very often. One time, though, I told them I saw *The Wizard of Oz*. I didn't know the names of the stars, but I thought one of them was called Dorothy. They looked disappointed, but we forgot about this and talked about other things.

When we were at the grocery store, a shopkeeper said hello to me, and I heard her say, "The United States stood side-by-side with the king and with Canada during the war, and they are our friend." That helped me to feel good about being here in Hillbrook. I felt that Canada was our friend too.

Every day before school began, we would all stand and face the flag of England. We would sing to the king. His name was George, and he lived in England. It didn't bother me to sing to him because I was living in his country. We don't have a queen or a king or anything like that in America. We have a president who took over for the first president when the first president died. At least, that was how I understood it. If we were asked to sing for our president, I would have, but no one did or asked me to.

In America, I told them that we said a pledge to our country's flag every day. We always placed our right hand over our hearts when we said the pledge. We also sang a song asking God to bless our country, which we really needed, and it always made me feel proud.

A few days later, our teacher taught a geography lesson. She told us that Canada and the United States are located in North America and that Mexico and several countries south of Mexico are located in Central America. South America is located south of Central America.

Many people call the United States "America," but all of the countries in our continent are really American countries. I had not thought of America as the name of our continent. I thought calling the United States of America just America was easier to say, but I was glad I learned something important this day.

The recess at this school was different from Wilson. At Wilson, when we had recess, we had bars to climb, swings, and other climbing things. Sometimes we would play kickball and other games where you played on a team. I wouldn't get picked early to be on a team, especially if the captain of the team was a boy. I thought it was because I was thin and looked weak. But most of the time when I was picked, I tried to play as hard as I could.

At Hillbrook grade school, we played lots of relay and racing games. All the grades would come out to recess at the same time. I wasn't tall, but I found I could run fast, so I liked the relay races.

One day at recess, I heard one of the older girls in my sister's class say, "That's the other American girl, Penny," meaning me. I didn't like being pointed out for any reason. I knew now I wasn't too different. I wasn't Canadian but that we were all American.

My birthday was coming soon. Aunt Martha said she was going to invite some girls my age over to our house for a party and would send out invitations. She also said since I was new to everyone, she would write, "Please no gifts," on the invitations. Aunt Martha also told me she and Uncle Harold would buy me a gift for each girl coming to the party and that I could pick out the gifts.

The next few days were so happy for me. Aunt Martha and I went to a store on Saturday to choose the gifts. One shelf in the store had glass figurines of all kinds with beautiful dresses of every color. She asked me if I liked them, and I told her, "Yes, very much." She asked me if I would like to have some of these and to pick out seven for my birthday.

I picked out seven figurines with different colored dresses. They were all so beautiful that it was difficult for me to pick. We took them home, and I had to wait for the party to see them again. It was so thrilling I could barely wait for the day.

The party day came, and it was as lovely as I had imagined. The six girls came. We had tea or milk, candy mints and cake, and then we played games. The girls all attended my class except one who was in the grade ahead of me. When it was time for me to open my presents, the girls gathered around me in a circle to watch. I was so excited.

As I unwrapped each present, everyone oohed and aahed. When they were all unwrapped, I handed each girl one to hold, and counting me, there were seven. We passed our figurines around the circle so we could see each one closely. Each figurine was beautiful with their dresses of different colored glass.

My favorite dress was a dark pink with flowers on the skirt. I had never had such a beautiful present before. But for some reason, it felt kind of selfish to have so many beautiful figurines. I thought the one favorite would have been enough. I never mentioned my thoughts to Aunt Martha and Uncle Harold because they were trying to help me not miss my family so much. They thought this lovely gift would help me to feel more at home with them.

After the party was over and all of my friends were gone, Uncle Harold brought in a small red-lined box. He told me I could keep the figurines in the box so they would not get broken. I thanked him and Aunt Martha and told them how much I loved them. I loved the figurines, but I was also beginning to love Aunt Martha and Uncle Harold too because they were so caring.

I put each figurine carefully into the fabric-lined box, but I knew I would not be able to keep them in the box very long. I would want to take them out of the box and look at them every day.

Later Margaret came into our room to see my gifts. She admired them for a moment and then pulled out from behind her skirt a small package. She handed the package to me. I opened it and saw that it was a pretty light blue ribbon with a heart charm on it. It was to be worn like a necklace.

"Happy Birthday," she said.

I loved the necklace and hugged and thanked her. Margaret always picked the prettiest things. I felt very proud to have such a grownup-looking necklace.

The next day, Aunt Martha told me that because I had had my birthday, I should have a checkup at the doctor. She said there was nothing wrong with me, but they thought that all children had checkups on their birthdays.

The doctor told Aunt Martha and Uncle Harold that I was small for my age and needed to gain some weight. He gave them some vitamin pills to give me to increase my appetite, but the pills didn't taste very good by themselves.

They didn't know, but I knew Aunt Martha was crushing the pills and covering them up by putting them in my rutabagas, which we ate a lot. I think the rutabagas were some of the vegetables stored in the cellar. I had seen Auntie crushing them and putting them in the rutabagas at one mealtime.

These pills were to help me grow taller and stronger. I didn't care if the vitamins were in the rutabagas because she put lots of butter on them, and I couldn't taste them. For some reason, I liked rutabagas, and I ate a lot of them.

The weather was getting warmer. Every day after school, Margaret wanted me to take a long walk down the road our parents would be driving on to get to Aunt Martha and Uncle Harold's house. Margaret hoped we would see them coming up the road. Some days I didn't want to take another walk with Margaret, but she begged me. She was so lonely and unhappy that I would always go with her.

As we were walking along, we would talk about all kinds of things. She would tell me about her friends at home and how she wished she could go home. I tried to change the subject, so I said, "How many years did you take piano lessons?"

Margaret said, "Almost six years, Penny. Why do you want to know that? I have thought about it." She continued, "And I really don't think I need more lessons. I have learned all I can from my teacher. I think it's really up to me. I won't be studying music in the university. When I graduate from high school, I want to become a teacher, like mother, and I can still play the piano."

"Margaret," I said, "you play so well now and play at church during singing in Sunday school. The reason I asked about your lessons was I asked Mother if I could take lessons, and she said, 'I don't think we can plan for that now. With your trip and the new baby coming, we'll have to wait and see after things return to normal.'"

Margaret smiled at me and said, "It's okay if you would like to take piano lessons, Penny. I really don't think I need more lessons. I just need new sheet music and maybe some new music books."

I looked at Margaret and thought how lucky I was to have such a practical, talented sister, but I didn't say anything. We were quiet for a few minutes. As we walked along the road, we often saw people in their yards and on the streets. They spoke and waved to us and were very friendly. I asked Margaret if she liked it here. She said she would if she had friends her own age like those at home. When I talked about how friendly people were here, always saying hello to us and smiling, she would nod but not with her heart. I felt if she could make some friends, she might change her mind about life in Canada.

When we would get to a certain place on the road, we would then turn around. We knew they wouldn't be arriving that day and that things had not changed very much at home.

Our parents called us regularly, usually on Sunday evenings. Sometimes they would only talk to Aunt Martha and Uncle Harold. Most of the time it helped us feel better to talk to Mother and Father, but sometimes afterward, we would feel lonelier.

# 6

# The Immigrant

One day, our teachers said there was to be an English holiday and that we would have no school. The next day, Aunt Martha told us she would be taking us to Saskatoon to buy some school and church clothes because "Easter is coming, and you are outgrowing yours."

We were going to drive to Saskatoon and stay overnight in the same hotel we had first stayed in with Uncle Harold. We were going to start out the next morning early. Aunt Martha said, "Saskatoon is larger than Hillbrook and has more stores and more options of clothing to pick from." I remembered Saskatoon from our journey before.

Early the next morning, Aunt Martha gathered Margaret, Henry, and me all together with our things and set off back to Saskatoon. Aunt Martha would be driving this time since Uncle Harold was busy and unable to come with us. He had to take care of some of his patients, plus he had church meetings and other group meetings in Hillbrook. I thought Aunt Martha wanted to give him time to go to the meetings and to "catch up on his work." Also, Uncle Harold was very nice, but he wasn't used to children. I just don't think he would have been able to keep up with us.

When we arrived in Saskatoon, we went directly to the hotel. Helpful people in the hotel told us it was called the Bessborough Hotel. They told us it was built by the Canadian railroad company to house passengers who wanted to spend some time in the city of Saskatoon. It was very beautiful with elevators, a big staircase, and dining rooms.

We went up the elevator to our room to wash our hands and comb our hair. Martha told us we were going to eat in the hotel dining room for dinner, and tomorrow morning, we would begin our shopping. She thought the town had more shoes and clothes to fit us, but she said, "It will take time to find all we need." She had already decided to stay two nights at the hotel so we could shop the next day, which was Saturday, and start home on Sunday.

On Saturday morning after breakfast in the big dining room, we all went shopping. I think I was right about Uncle Harold. He would not have been able to keep up with us. We went to all the stores and only stopped for lunch. Each one of us bought new shoes and clothes after trying on everything. Even Aunt Martha purchased some things for herself and said she would mail them back to the store if they didn't fit. Margaret explained to me that Aunt Martha didn't want to take the time to try things on for herself.

Henry began to get tired in the late afternoon. He asked when we were going to eat, and Martha told us we would have dinner again in the dining room that evening. We were all very tired when we sat down to dinner, especially Aunt Martha. We ate chicken, mashed potatoes, and pie for dessert, just like our first day in Canada. Only this time, the pie was called Wild Blueberry. "Wild blueberries grow easily in Canada," Martha said. They are smaller than the blueberries I had in Kansas City but were just as delicious. The pie had fluffy whipped cream on top of it.

The dining room was as nice as I remembered with white tablecloths, napkins, and fresh flowers on the table. The ladies who waited on us were very polite and explained to us the dishes they had available and those we had ordered. This way, Martha told us we would know if we would eat the dishes we ordered. I thought this was a good idea. Of course, I ate all of my dinner. In fact, we all did, even Henry!

With our shopping over for the day, we decided to take a short walk outside the hotel. There were pretty flower gardens in the back of the hotel on the path where we walked and along the pathway near the Saskatchewan River. There were many people walking alongside the river.

The ladies wore their pretty long dresses that rustled when they walked.

The evening air made us all yawn. After a short walk, Henry asked Aunt Martha, "When are we going back to our room?"

Martha looked at all of us and said, "The sun is setting, and we will have a long drive home tomorrow. Let's start back to the hotel to our rooms. Tomorrow will come quickly after our heads hit our pillows."

Margaret and I didn't object. We were both tired, and it had been a lovely day. Later, even Margaret said she had enjoyed it. The next day was Sunday. We got up early, and after breakfast, Aunt Martha checked out of the hotel to start the trip back home. From the hotel lobby, I thought I saw the same older man I had seen before in the train station in Kansas City sitting at a breakfast table. I wasn't sure he was the same man, but he looked a lot like him. He was there eating breakfast with another young woman.

Just then, when the young woman left the gentleman's table and headed toward the restroom, I told Aunt Martha I had to go to the bathroom. She said it was a good idea for all of us to go, if we needed, before we started the long trip home. Margaret didn't want to go, so I told Aunt Martha I could go by myself and would be back in a minute. She told me to go on but to hurry back.

When I got to the restroom, I waited in the stall for the young lady to come out and go up to a sink and mirror.

When I heard her washing her hands, I quickly flushed and went to the sink. She was looking in the mirror, combing her hair. Then she took off a necklace chain she had been wearing around her neck. It had been covered by her clothing. I noticed on the chain there was a ring. It had a lady's face carved in white with a black background. It was just like the other lady's ring in the Union Station in Kansas City.

I stared at it and then at her but quickly said, "Oh, what a pretty ring."

She thanked me. I said I was new to the town and asked if she lived here. She said, "I've just arrived. I will be here a little while, but I don't know how long I will live here." The young lady smiled at me, but her eyes were not smiling. They seemed to be kind of reddish and moist, like she had been crying.

I didn't want to ask her more questions, even though I was very curious. Her voice had a strange sound to it. I had never heard this accent before. It wasn't the English I knew. The young lady started talking again. She said she had traveled a long way and that now she would have to stop for a while. I knew Aunt Martha would be worried, so I told her I had to go but that I hoped she would find her way again. She smiled, thanked me, and said good-bye as I left.

I went back to the lobby to meet Aunt Martha, Margaret, and Henry where they were waiting for me. The young woman came out of the restroom. As we were going to the door to leave the hotel, the young woman also left with the older gentleman and passed us at the front door of the hotel.

Our automobile was parked close by, and since we were ready to go, we piled into the car for the journey home. The ride back to Hillbrook seemed to take a long time. Aunt Martha drove the car with very few stops along the way. We kept as quiet as we could and took naps to help the time pass quickly.

As we rode the long journey home, I thought about the lady I had met in the hotel restroom. She said she had come a long way, so maybe she was new to Canada and spoke a different form of English. Perhaps that was why her voice sounded strange to me. Maybe she was an immigrant. America had many of these people. This was a new word I had learned in one of the books Mother had bought for us. It was a word my teacher at school had used in our history class.

Many immigrants came to America when our country was brand-new. Mother said they came for freedom, which is what my teacher also said. I was not sure what that means, but maybe it means to be able to walk where you want and to speak to all your neighbors. I had heard speakers on the radio talking about more people coming to live in the United States now the war was over.

I wondered why the lady in the hotel had a ring like the other woman in the train station in Kansas City. Both ladies had dark hair, and even though one looked older, they did look alike. It was a mystery to me, though, that one young woman had a strange-sounding voice and the other didn't.

I guessed I probably wouldn't see them again, but I hoped this young woman would find her way and soon be happier. The long drive made me feel tired. Even though I kept thinking about these two strange ladies, I gradually fell asleep.

We were very glad when we arrived in Hillbrook. Uncle Harold seemed cheerful and relieved to have us home. We ate our dinner and took a bath for bed.

That night, as I climbed into bed and began to fall asleep, my dreams were full of the events of the weekend. It all became a mystery I didn't know how to solve.

In school the next day, I found myself daydreaming a lot. After recess, I began to forget my troubles and started to pay more attention in class. Things seemed to get back to normal.

# 7

# Lisa

Lisa didn't understand exactly why her visa had not been approved. She would be staying in Canada until all of the details could be worked out and all of her applications approved. Then she could move to the United States.

She knew she had problems without sponsors. She had an aunt and uncle who lived there, but she couldn't remember her uncle's last name. She was very young when they married and moved to the United States. She remembered her uncle was an engineer and that her aunt, her mother's sister, was a teacher like her mother. They had decided to apply to the United States when the news they heard was full of the threatening direction the war was taking. They became fearful, especially since her uncle was Jewish.

The aunt and uncle wrote letters to the family from America, but gradually communication from them stopped. Lisa and her family were no longer receiving mail. She was a young student, and her sister had just graduated from the Catholic school where her mother and Kathleen, her mother's friend, had taught. Her sister, Lauren, had skipped the eighth grade and was to begin her university studies early.

When living in France continued to be difficult, Lisa's mother made the decision to send Lisa to England. Kathleen, working as a teacher in her mother's school, had decided to leave France and return to England and eventually Ireland, her homeland. Fearing for Lisa's safety, Lisa's mother planned to send Lisa to England in the safe keeping of her friend and fellow teacher, Kathleen. This was in 1938. Lisa was only eleven years old.

Soon the planning began for the best opportunity to travel. Lisa and Kathleen, with the help of friends, were to travel to England. First by ship and upon arrival in England, the completion of the journey was to be determined by Kathleen's family and friends and the activities of the war. Ultimately, their goal was to reach Dublin, Ireland, Kathleen's homeland.

After they left by ship, Lauren never heard from Lisa or any of Kathleen's family or friends regarding where they were. The occupation of Paris prohibited the freedom of communication, and little was reaching either country.

After a few days of travel by land in England, Lisa and Kathleen crossed over to Ireland by way of a ferry, where they arrived in Dublin, Kathleen's home. Friends who took them in and along this journey helped to ease their concerns with their encouragement and loving care.

Upon arriving in Dublin, Kathleen's family took Lisa into their home with loving arms. They cared for her physical needs, took her to church, and helped her to enroll in school. The main problem she experienced was the language differences. Gradually, she began to learn, and since many also spoke English, she soon adapted.

*This must be what immigrants everywhere in the world must feel when they are in a foreign land and can't speak the languages*, she told herself. *I am so fortunate to have so many friends here to help me.*

After several years, when the war was over, Lisa, encouraged by Kathleen and her family, began to consider moving to the United States to locate her aunt and uncle, the only members of her family she had left. She was so young when she left France with Kathleen.

She had been with Kathleen's family for more than six years. They understood how much she had loved her family. It was a very difficult decision she would make to leave Kathleen, her family, and the new friends and life she had made. She loved them all and knew she would miss them. She felt like a member of their family.

When the war had ended, they began to encourage her to think ahead and to go to the United States to try to find her aunt and uncle. Lisa cared for her family in Ireland very much, and yet she needed to find her remaining family as well, she told herself, if possible. She was very sad to leave her Irish family. They told her on the day she left on her journey, "It is up to you to choose where home is, but first try to find your family in America. Please remember, we love you, and you'll always be welcome here."

All of Lisa's family was gone now except her mother's sister and husband in America. She felt it was almost a lost cause looking for them in such a large country—except she had some memories from their letters.

In the beginning, the few letters they had received had described land and farms with crops and nice, friendly people. They said they felt comfortable in the areas they lived in because of the people. Lisa also remembered something about the middle part of the country. She decided to look in the areas of the Midwest where farming was common and to work with the agencies who were trying to reunite war-torn families.

Lisa came into North America by way of Canada from Ireland. She was working with one Catholic group active in helping to unite families separated by the war. She stayed in Canada for a while. Many people were trying to enter the United States now the war was over usually to join family members. She might be here for some time unfortunately until she could immigrate to America. She told herself to keep trying and to not give up hope.

She had been given information to contact Mr. Cowan and a group of Roman Catholic priests in this area who helped families reconnect from Europe to Canada and then to the United States. He recommended she find some work in the area when she was unable to move on. Without names and information regarding her family in the United States, she may be here in Canada for some time, and she only had a work visa for so long in Canada.

Years before, when she left France with Kathleen, her mother had given her a ring to wear. The ring was given to her mother by Lisa's father. It was too big for Lisa to wear on her finger at that time, so her mother had put it on a chain to wear around her neck.

It had been more than six years ago, and now she was able to wear it on her finger. She took off the chain, removed the ring, and placed the ring on her finger. Her mother had told her she would have been given a ring like this one when she graduated from the eighth grade, like her sister, Lauren. When this wasn't going to happen, her mother went ahead and gave her the ring. This was a precious ring to Lisa.

This day, Lisa found out she wasn't going on to her destination in America. However, in spite of this disappointment, she decided to put the ring on and to be positive and hopeful that she would eventually find her aunt and uncle in America. Many were working with other groups to help her continue the search.

# 8

# New Friends

Now that my birthday was over and I was a year older, I was looking forward to the next adventure. Margaret and I kept up our walks, but the baby still hadn't come. We knew we wouldn't see Mother and Father's automobile on the road very soon.

With the days getting warmer, we began to play outdoors in the evening, especially croquet in our side yard before dinner. One evening at dinner, we had a new guest. Her name was Eileen.

Eileen was helping Aunt Martha by cleaning and preparing our meals. She was a good cook and sometimes would bring the food to the table and serve us like they did in the hotel. I asked her one day why she ate in the kitchen and not with us in the dining room. She told me she liked eating in the kitchen and that she was paid to work in our house. Every day she would come early to prepare breakfast and stayed to do other housework. She said it was a lot of work to have children. I asked Eileen if she had children. She said no but that someday she hoped she would.

I learned several new things about Eileen. She told us she was a member of another church from ours and that her family was Roman Catholic. She was the oldest child of five children and helped her mother and father with the others. After her sixteenth birthday, she had stopped going to school. She had planned to find a job and was happy to have a job with Martha and Harold.

She was very talented. She could cook, clean, polish shoes, sew, and do lots of other jobs. Sometimes she would use Aunt Martha's sewing machine to mend clothes. She told us she was making a crocheted cover for her bed at her parents' home.

Eileen told Margaret and me that she had a friend who had been a soldier in the war and that he was coming home soon. She and the soldier were members of the same church. He was a few years older. When the war came and he was no longer in school, he was called to serve in the Royal Navy. He said he had come home on leave and that "they spent time together as much time as he had." They had been writing letters when he went back on duty to the battleship. Later the ship was attacked. He was sent to a hospital because he had been injured, but she said, "He is on the mend."

When Eileen began telling us about her friend's injury, she suddenly stopped talking and changed the subject. She asked if we would like some new play clothes for summer because we would be "easy to sew for." She was even going to try to make some play clothes for Henry. We said yes, and she began bringing new material to the house and sewing new play clothes for all of us.

Margaret liked Eileen a lot because she wasn't much older than herself. Sometimes they would talk and laugh. I thought that Margaret began to feel better because Eileen was here. Aunt Martha was also glad Eileen was here because Aunt Martha was able to help in Uncle Harold's office while Eileen was busy with us.

Martha liked working with Harold's patients, and the patients seemed glad to see her. Aunt Martha would answer the door, speak on the telephone, and do paperwork. Sometimes she would take the money or whatever the patients gave her for Uncle Harold's work. When the patients didn't have any or enough money to pay for his work, Harold would say, "You can pay when you have it."

I was worried that taking care of all three of us might cost Martha and Harold a lot of money. Margaret and I felt grateful to them for caring for us. They were buying us clothes, feeding us, and caring for all our needs like our own mother and father. I thought they would have liked having children of their own as Aunt Martha and Uncle Harold treated us like their own. I hoped they would become parents someday because it would be easy for them. They already knew how.

Aunt Martha had company sometimes. She and her friends drank tea and would dress up in nice clothes and talk a lot. I had seen some of them at church.

One day after school, I brought a friend home to play. She was thirsty, and I brought her into our house for a glass of water. When we entered the front door, I saw Martha's friends sitting in the parlor, talking. I told my friend to be very quiet and to not disturb them as we walked through the hall to the kitchen. Martha said hello to me, and I said, "Please excuse us. My friend was thirsty, and I was going to get her a drink."

I looked around the room of ladies. Some of the ladies looked as though they might be thirsty, so I said, "Would anyone else like a drink?" One of the ladies said, "No, thank you," and smiled. As we passed on to the kitchen, I heard her say, "What nice manners she has." And then the talking started up again.

We left the house for the yard by the back door in the kitchen as Eileen gave me some cookies. Margaret, who was in the kitchen with Eileen, said, "I'll go with you to walk your friend home when you're ready." But I knew she had said this because she wanted to walk down the road again looking for Mother and Father's Chevrolet.

There wasn't much to tell about my brother, Henry. He was very sweet and always behaved well—at least, it seemed so to me. He had light reddish-blond hair, and his skin was pale like mine, but he was a little chubby. I could tell Martha and Harold liked him. Since they didn't have children, they probably wished they had a son like him. They dressed him up to look like a little prince, and the people at church gushed over his sweet looks and good nature. Aunt Martha's eyes would seem to light up each time.

Aunt Martha and Uncle Harold attended a different church than we did in the United States. It was the Church of England, which was my father's real church. Mother's church was called the Christian Church, and at home, all of us went there. My father went once in a while with the family, but he didn't go very often.

Both of my father's brothers and sister went to the Church of England, which was called the Episcopal Church in the United States. Now because we were in Canada, we attended the Church of England. It was different, and it took some time for me to learn their way of praying. Margaret said she did not like the church that much, but she knew there was a boy in the church that liked her.

Margaret looked very different from me. She was tall with thick blond hair, was very smart, and a lot of fun. The boy who liked Margaret was named Farley. He tried to speak to her and talk to her at church. Aunt Martha didn't like Margaret talking to him. Martha thought Margaret was too young to talk to boys, even though Farley was the same age and polite.

Margaret, however, began to like Farley and tried to talk to him whenever she could without Aunt Martha knowing. Farley was in her Sunday school class, which was one place they could talk that Martha would not know about. The class also met on Wednesday evenings for worship and Bible studies.

Margaret soon began to like going to church on Wednesday evening. Martha would send me along with Margaret. I thought maybe she wanted me to watch them and let her know what they were doing. I didn't tell Aunt Martha about all the times they talked or laughed together. I didn't think it was wrong to have fun at church. Farley asked if he could come to the house to visit Margaret, but she was shy about asking Martha and Harold's permission. Margaret began to act a little happier at this time.

The weather was getting warmer, and light jackets or sweaters were all we needed. Uncle Harold and Aunt Martha told us about Loon Lake. They said when the weather got warmer, they often went to Loon Lake for picnics and to fish.

It was quite a drive from Hillbrook. If the weather permitted, they would take food to a small cabin they used to stay all night. They said they wanted to invite our Sunday school classes to Loon Lake for an afternoon picnic later on. They also said they would pick a Sunday when the weather would be warm and asked if we would like to learn to fish. Of course, we said yes.

We were so excited about going there and having a picnic with our church and school friends. Lots of people in our town knew about Loon Lake. It was a vacation place the town people went to in the summer when the weather got warmer. I thought it was called Loon Lake because of the many birds called loons that lived there.

Margaret's birthday was in June, the same month our new baby sister or brother was going to be born. She was going to be fourteen years old. Martha and Harry said that this would be a perfect time for a picnic at Loon Lake to celebrate Margaret's birthday. They also said we could learn to fish in the boats on the lake or off the side of the bank. Margaret and I thought it really sounded exciting.

At Loon Lake, they told us a larger main cabin had lots of wooden seats and tables. It also had a movie projector for showing movies. Some of the people that lived at the lake in the summer ran the movie projector. They charged a small fee for everyone visiting at the lake to see the movies. Margaret thought Farley might be able to come to the picnic, and maybe they could both see the movies together.

Uncle Harry said that I could go out on a boat with him to fish if I wanted to, but he said Henry was too little. He wouldn't be able to fish out on a boat, but he could fish off the bank, and Uncle Harold would help him.

Soon school would be over for the year, and we could celebrate with a picnic at Loon Lake. Aunt Martha and Uncle agreed. "After we see the lake and cabins together, it would be easier for us to make plans for Margaret's birthday."

Loon Lake sounded so exciting to us. Then Aunt Martha told us Hillbrook was having their annual town fair very soon. I didn't know what a town fair was because I had never been to one. With the trip to Loon Lake and a town fair to go to, I wasn't sure I could wait for it all to happen!

# 9

# Town Fair

An article about the town fair appeared in bold print in the Hillbrook weekly newspaper. The fair was to be held at all of the churches and in the town square with all the towns people invited. Martha told us, "This is an event to celebrate the graduation from eighth grade and high school that takes place annually at the end of May."

Aunt Martha told us that each church group organized fund-raising games and other projects. The ladies would bring their favorite canned and baked goods to be judged and then purchased. There would be handmade quilts, hooked rugs, clothing, knitted socks, and sweaters, along with blankets and many other crafts, for sale. Some of the proceeds were to be given to the churches. Some major cash prizes would be for academic awards to be given to the high school graduates with the highest grades. These awards would help give financial assistance to students planning to attend the universities in Canada. Uncle Harold told us, "The University in Toronto has a fine dental college."

We were all very excited to be able to go to a town fair since we had never been to one. With the Loon Lake visit coming as well, we were very anxious about waiting for it all to happen.

Margaret and I were not taking the walks to the "road" as much as before. Life in Canada was feeling more like home, and Margaret even said, "I hope they don't come for us for a while. It will be very hard to leave here. I can see now that living in a small town can be good. You know everyone, you can walk everywhere, and the people are so friendly."

I was thinking the same thoughts, but I just smiled at her. She didn't mention Farley.

The day of the fair came. We dressed in the new play clothes Eileen had made for us, and then we hurried to the nearest event. Aunt Martha told Margaret and me to stay together, while she and Harold walked around the fair with Henry.

We went to our church first anticipating the expected pancake breakfast. We got in the long line as soon as we could. When our turn came, we held out our plates for yummy hot pancakes with gobs of butter and maple syrup.

Farley saw Margaret, waved, came, and sat with us. Eating with them began to feel like I was alone because they looked only at each other while talking and laughing constantly. I knew she didn't want to have me with them, but Aunt and Uncle would not approve if I left them.

After eating our delicious pancakes, we started looking at the other church events. A few of the judges were there tasting some of the food items made by several of the townspeople. The fruit pies and jams looked so delicious; I hoped Aunt Martha would buy some for us to have at home.

Margaret found some pretty things right away, but I wanted to look at as many of the booths as I could with things for sale so I could then decide what I wanted to buy. I had saved my money for this day and wanted to get the best item I could find.

I saw two of my Sunday school girl classmates, and we then decided to visit the booths together. As I talked with my friends, I saw Aunt Martha and Uncle Harold in line for pancakes with Henry. Knowing how long it would take them to get their food and finish, especially since they had seen some of their friends and would do a lot of talking, we decided to move on quickly.

My friends and I went to other churches to visit some of their booths for sale items. Margaret and Farley decided to leave for some of the other exhibits. We said we would meet in the square in one hour.

After seeing everything in one other church, my friends took me to some of the exhibits in the town square. We saw some things we wanted to buy, but everything was more expensive than we could afford.

Then I saw some beautiful boxes with colorful flowers and birds on them at a booth close by. I moved over quickly to look at them. The boxes were round and decorated in what the lady behind the booth called papier-mâché. The prints were all scenes of flower gardens and had lids that sat on top. They were handmade and would make a perfect gift.

I asked the lady behind the table how much one would cost. She asked me how much money I had to spend, and I told her what I had, and she said that was exactly what she was charging. So I bought a box. I asked the lady if she had a bag I could put the box in because it was to be a surprise. She found a big bag, and now no one except my friends would know what was in the bag.

I had been away from Margaret for about an hour and knew I should find her and Farley before Aunt and Uncle saw them together without me. When I turned around to look for them, Margaret and Farley came up to us.

We all began to look some more at all of the items for sale when someone announced the awards would be given in fifteen minutes. We rushed to the stage on the square, which was set up for the ceremony. We found seats for all of us up front to see the winners receiving their awards. I looked for Aunt Martha, Uncle Harold, and Henry but didn't see them.

The headmaster of the school was the person in charge of this event. He walked onto the small stage to greet everyone in the audience. One by one, he called the six winners to the stage to acknowledge their accomplishments and announce the amount of cash awards they would receive.

All of the winners were very grateful, and each expressed their appreciation by saying they would be continuing their education with the help of the awards. Some of their grade scores were so high I was amazed. It must have taken a lot of studying for the winners to achieve their honors. When I said, "The audience is clapping a lot for them," Margaret replied, "This is for their financial help."

It was at this time I thought that if I worked harder on my schoolwork, maybe I could do better like my teacher said when school was to be over for the summer. I would try harder next year at my school in Kansas City. This thought made me feel surprisingly sick to my stomach. What if I couldn't do better? I should talk to Margaret about what my teacher said about this. I decided to wait and think about it later and then talk to Margaret. It was still summer, and we had a lot to look forward to.

The afternoon was starting to cool down. I was beginning to think it was time for us to go home, especially me and my friends. I said good-bye to my two friends and, carrying my box in a big sack, started home. Margaret saw I was leaving and said good-bye to Farley so she could arrive at Aunt Martha and Uncle Harold's home with me.

It was a fun day, but I was very tired and wanted to get home to hide my package. Margaret didn't even ask what I had in the bag. I didn't want anyone to know what I had purchased. I really wanted to keep it a secret for now.

# 10

# Loon Lake

The days were getting warmer. It felt like summer vacation should begin soon. My skirt was always sticking to me at the end of the day, so I couldn't wait to get home to change into my play clothes and get outside where the breezes would cool me. I was ready for school to be out today. Then I heard the most terrible news!

Our teacher told us that the test we would have tomorrow would be the last one for this year and to "take home your notes and study hard for the test and do the best you can." She also said she would grade them tomorrow while we had a long recess. Tomorrow during recess, there were going to be lots of games and prizes given. When recess was over, she would give us our grade cards, and we would be dismissed until next year's classes.

Well, my stomach began to turn over, and I felt nauseous. I was going to go home tomorrow, and next fall, I wouldn't be coming back to this school. I wouldn't be here to sing to the king or run relays and play outside with my friends. Even though my clothes were sticking to me, I didn't care. I didn't want to go to school the next day, but Aunt Martha said I should go.

"Go to school and say good-bye to your teacher and friends you won't see the rest of the summer," she said. She gave me a couple of small presents to take to my teacher and the principal, and I finished my year at the English school.

With the end of school, however, our summer adventures began. Margaret and I walked all over Hillbrook, taking our time and talking to everyone who would talk back. We started planning our trip to Loon Lake and what we would do at Margaret's birthday party. She would be fourteen years old and wanted to invite Farley.

I was pretty sure Aunt Martha would not allow boys to come, but Margaret said she would try to talk to Aunt Martha and Uncle Harold about it. After all, Margaret said, she would soon be going home to America, and she was now fourteen years old! It sounded like a good plan, but I was glad I didn't have to ask them.

The first trip to Loon Lake was to see everything at the lake. There were cabins families stayed in, beaches for lounging, and the lake for swimming, fishing, and boating. I really didn't like swimming in the lake because the bottom was muddy, and sometimes I could feel little fish or weeds rubbing against my legs. But I liked the sound of boat fishing in the lake and fishing off of the docks, so there was plenty to do!

We saw the cabin in which they showed movies. They were usually cowboy movies. *Hopalong Cassidy* was one very popular cowboy movie I knew because he helped people. He always wore black, and his horse named Topper was white. I thought Hopalong was a very handsome cowboy mainly because he was a thoughtful and kind person who was good to his horse and rustlers who were sorry. However, sometimes rustlers went to jail when he settled the problems. Sometimes, Topper, his smart white horse, could do many tricks and saved Hopalong just in time when he was in trouble. I hoped we would see a cowboy movie.

Uncle Harold said he would go out on the boat to fish with me but that I had to wear a life jacket. So we got all of our gear and got into the boat. He asked if I wanted to put the worms on the hook, but I said he could do that if he wanted to! He also said the person that caught the most fish would get a dollar. I caught two fish, but he kept throwing his catch back into the lake, saying they were too small. We ended up with just my two big fish. Uncle Harold said he would pay me later, and I said okay.

We started to get tired and warm from being out on the water in the afternoon sun, so we decided to go back to the shore. Aunt Martha and Margaret were packing up everything to go to the cabin. Uncle Harold said he would teach Henry to fish tomorrow off the side of the lake. They told us if we hurried and ate dinner at the cabin, we might be able to see a movie.

We hurried back and cooked and then ate our dinner of the fish I had caught. They were very tasty. Uncle Harold made a big fuss about me catching the most fish but never mentioned the one dollar he owed me. I decided not to say anything about it.

After dinner, we all combed our hair and headed over to the movie cabin. There were several people there. Some of the people of the North called Inuits were there. They were very friendly, speaking to us and smiling. They knew Aunt Martha and Uncle Harold, as some of them had been to our house in Hillbrook for dental work.

It was my lucky day because a *Hopalong Cassidy* movie was showing. Everyone cheered when Hopalong lassoed the rustlers and put them in jail. They had stolen someone's cattle and wouldn't give them back. We knew that just wasn't right!

After the movie, we said good night to everyone and went back to our cabin. It had been a full day. We all went to bed and slept easily until the sun came up.

That morning after breakfast, Margaret and I took a walk around the lake. It was too big for us to walk all the way around, but we saw lots of little squirrels and birds along the path we took. The fish were jumping out of the water. Many people were fishing off the side of the lake and in boats.

Margaret and I talked about her asking about Farley coming to the birthday picnic. She hadn't asked yet but said she hoped she would be able to. Martha and Harold were still fishing with Henry, so Margaret and I went swimming after our walk. I wore socks with rubber bands around the tops to hold them up when we were swimming, but it didn't help much; I could still feel the squishy muddy bottom when I set my feet down.

After a late lunch, Uncle Harold said we should pack our things and head back to Hillbrook. We had a fun weekend, and now we were thinking about coming back to Loon Lake for the birthday picnic.

# 11

## Boys at the Birthday Party

Margaret was waiting for a good time to ask Aunt Martha and Uncle Harold about an invitation for Farley to her picnic. She thought since she was going to be fourteen and would be leaving to go home soon, they might consent. But she thought they might not like Farley or think she was too young to invite boys to a party. She just didn't know what they would say, so every day she put off asking.

Then one day, I asked her again if she had talked to Aunt Martha. She had to tell me no again. She said she felt so angry at herself, so she decided today was going to be the day no matter what!

Later in the day, Margaret told me she had decided to talk to Aunt Martha about inviting Farley to her birthday party. She continued telling me Martha was in the dining room writing out a list for her shopping.

"Aunt Martha," Margaret had said.

Martha raised her head up from her writing and said, "Oh, Margaret, I need to talk to you. You will need to write out a list of your friends' names so I can write the invitations to your birthday picnic. Will you do that for me as soon as today? I'm going shopping, and you should go with me to help pick out the invitations and your party favors. Do you think this Saturday would be a good day for the picnic? The weather looks good, and we have just enough days ahead to send the invitations out and hear back."

Margaret told me she was overwhelmed for a minute but had managed to say, "This coming Saturday would be perfect, Aunt Martha. I'll make the list right now."

She felt the time to ask about Farley was upon her. Getting up the courage and clearing her throat, she asked, "Would it be possible for me to invite a couple of boys from my Sunday school? I was thinking of asking Farley and his brother, James. James is one year younger but acted very mature. Also, I would like to ask all of the girls in my Sunday school class. That would be eight, including Penny and me. Is that too many?"

Aunt Martha thought quietly. "Hmm," she said, "six girls and two boys. That sounds about right. Go ahead and write down their names, and then I can post the invitations today."

"Oh, thank you, Aunt Martha. It all sounds so wonderful!" Margaret said.

Aunt Martha smiled and continued writing her list.

Margaret was walking on air the next couple of days. We continued our walks every day, but Margaret kept hoping we would *not* see our Chevrolet coming up the road. She said, "This party will be the best party I've ever had." Margaret told me she would tell me more good news later.

Her birthday was coming before Saturday. I thought about when I should give Margaret her surprise gift. I decided to go up this evening after dinner and ask her to come too. My box for Margaret was so big I could only wrap it in some leftover paper used to wrap clothes for storage. I tied a pretty white ribbon around it. I had a nice card for her on which I had written a message. I hoped she would like it.

When dinner was over, Margaret and I excused ourselves and went up to our bedroom. She didn't ask me why we were going up there by ourselves. Aunt Martha and Uncle Harold said we would have a family party tomorrow evening with cake to celebrate Margaret's birthday.

I think Margaret thought I wanted to have a small celebration between the two of us, so she didn't say anything when I asked her to join me after dinner. When I gave her the present and card, Margaret had tears in her eyes. She said she adored the box." It is so pretty with all of the colorful flowers on it. I'll have a place to put all of my private treasures. Thank you, Penny."

She opened the card with the poem I had written. It said:

> My sister is my special friend,
> no better one to ask for.
> She takes good care of me each day,
> I could not want for more.

"That's a lovely poem, Penny. Thank you," Margaret said as she hugged me. Excitedly, she continued, "I have thought more about the birthday party to talk to you about. Because Aunt Martha agreed to have Farley and James to the party, we will have some more planning to do!"

I was happy for Margaret. James was very nice too and always makes me laugh. I decided this party was going to be the best ever. Actually, this was the first real party I had ever attended with boys included!

Aunt Martha mailed the invitations and began receiving telephone calls from the mothers asking for details as soon as the invitations were delivered to their homes.

"Yes of course," she would say. "We will be with them at the lake. No, they will not be *in* the lake. No, they will not be swimming. Only Harold and Henry will be close to the lake. They are going to be fishing off the bank of the lake. Harold and I will be driving everyone to Loon Lake. I have friends who will drive also. Everyone will arrive together at the same time."

After a pause, she would ask, "So she can come? That's wonderful! We'll call with the time we will pick her up. See you soon."

Margaret and I knew this was a new experience for Aunt Martha, but we thought she did a good job of organizing and answering the concerns of the parents. We talked about the possibility that our own mother may not have done a better job and that it was too bad that Martha didn't have any children of her own.

These plans were coming together nicely, but now we needed to put our heads together to come up with games and food to serve. It would be the best party any of us had ever attended. Margaret and I decided we would need to build a campfire with Uncle Harold's help, and then we would be able to roast marshmallows. Aunt Martha said she would make fried chicken and potato salad and bring some fresh fruit, lemonade, and, of course, the cake. Maybe some cookies for later for the drive home, she said.

On the day of the party, Aunt Martha, who had asked a couple of her friends to help, started picking up the friends, making a caravan. Uncle Harold led the caravan with a friend of his helping him by driving the last car. Loon Lake was a couple hours' drive away, so we decided to sing songs and play quiz games to fill the time.

Farley and his brother were in a friend's car. I could tell Margaret was very excited about getting to the lake because she kept asking how far it was and how long it would take before we would arrive.

When we finally arrived at Loon Lake, it looked so beautiful and green. The weather was perfect, and as we got out of the car, Aunt and Uncle, together with their friends, began to unload all of the equipment. Farley and James helped to set things up. I think Aunt Martha and Uncle Harold were pleased they wanted to help, especially with the campfire.

Farley and James started to light the fire with Uncle Harold's help, while Aunt Martha began to set out all of the food and drink. She said because the trip was long, we could eat first and then start the party games after. She laid the cloth on a table with the food and drinks, and even the cake. We began filling our plates after our vicar said a grace. Everything tasted so delicious. Margaret and I said later the beautiful weather and cooler breezes made us hungry, especially the boys.

We roasted marshmallows after eating dinner. Aunt Martha said we would have the cake now if everyone wanted it. The cookies would be served later just before we started the return trip home. Of course, we wanted the cake now. It was white cake with a fluffy white icing, and it looked so delicious.

I was full to bursting after all the food, but Margaret said we should start playing games while we had sunshine and the really pleasant weather. We began with "Pin the Tail on the Donkey." Then we played hide-and-seek, which allowed us to wander more into the woods.

Finally, we had the scavenger hunt. Margaret had made lists of things we would need to find, forming teams of two persons each. With eight persons, there were four teams. The items would be found in the woods.

After we divided into teams, Margaret passed out our lists to everyone. She said we would give prizes to the first team to find the most items on the list and second prize to the next team with the second most items, and we would have thirty minutes to find them. Uncle Harold had loaned us an old hourglass. We turned it upside down and the search began!

I partnered with a friend, Caroline, from church. Margaret was with Farley, and James was with another girl, Janet, a year ahead of me in school. The last group was Joyce and her little sister, Lynnette, from church.

Uncle Harold and his friend, along with his friend's son, found a bank close by, and they started showing Henry and the other younger boy, Daniel, how to hold a fishing pole and all of the things they should know to start fishing. Aunt Martha, the vicar, and his wife, along with their friends, set up their chairs and, with their drinks—which I thought was tea—began to visit. It was the first time I had seen the vicar and his wife laugh. I was glad to see they could have fun. I thought they needed it.

Caroline and I started running around looking for our items. We decided to go further into the wooded area to find some of our things on the list. We were running so hard I began to get very hot, but we still looked hard to find our items. When Caroline and I heard Aunt Martha ring a bell, telling us that time was up, we panicked! We hadn't found one of the items.

When we got back to the campsite, my hair and clothes were sticking to me. Because I had slipped and lost my footing, I had some dirt on my hands and face. When Aunt Martha saw me, she took out a washcloth she had packed away and started to wipe some of the dirt off of me.

Margaret looked embarrassed when she saw what Aunt Martha was doing. Aunt Martha saw Margaret looking at her and stopped wiping off my face. Everyone else kept doing what they had been doing, so no one paid any attention to me and Aunt Martha.

Farley and Margaret won the first prize, while Farley's brother, James, with his partner, won second. They won free ice cream sundaes at the drugstore on the square in Hillbrook. They liked their prizes and thanked Aunt Martha and Uncle Harold for it. I thought James and Farley won because they were older, but I didn't really care because it was fun running around. Margaret should have won because it was her birthday.

We all had something to drink and then decided to play tag. Somehow, tag didn't seem as much fun as we thought it would be, so we decided to walk around the lake instead and maybe look for the movie building. Aunt Martha and her friends decided to come along in case we got lost.

There were quite a few people at the lake enjoying their vacation homes. There were many boats on the lake and people fishing. It was starting to feel cooler, so everyone began to put on their jackets and sweaters. It was just then that we saw the movie cabin. We ran to the movie building hoping there would be a movie playing we could see. We found enough chairs and sat down. A man stood up and said he had a Tom Mix movie he could show us if we wanted to see it.

Everyone cheered, and he began to thread the reel and show the film. It was the best film I had ever seen! The cowboys were able to do many tricks on their horses while riding very fast. This was good because they needed to ride fast in order to catch the cattle rustlers.

Tom Mix was the lawman, and he told the rustlers he would let them go if they would bring back the cattle they had stolen. But they wouldn't do that, so they had to go to jail. Finally, the rustlers said they were sorry, so the movie had a good ending, and everyone applauded!

I thought we would see cowboys and Indians fighting in the movie. Farley said they didn't show Indians fighting against cowboys in this movie house because Indians own the land this lake is on. They like their people shown as peaceful people, not warriors.

I asked if the man running the movie projector was an Eskimo, but Farley said, "No, he is an Indian. Many years ago when this land was beginning to be farmed by white people, this area had Indian tribes already here. Indians have been on this land for hundreds of years. They gave up a lot for white men to come here to live."

I learned a lot about people that day. Number one, Farley was smarter than I thought he was. Second, you can't learn about people until you spend time with them and they have to tell you their ideas. Then you have to think about their ideas and decide what you think about them. It doesn't really matter what you think about their ideas because they have a right to them as you have a right to yours. You can accept their ideas if you want—or not.

It was getting late, so we decided to head back to our campsite. Aunt and Uncle began to put things together to carry to the cars for the trip home. Cookies and lemonade were sitting out for all to take.

Everyone helped load up the cars and grabbed cookies and a drink for the ride home. We finished loading up and said good-bye to all for the day. We thanked Aunt Martha and Uncle Harold for a great day! I fell asleep on the way home. I was very grateful when we arrived, and I could lie down in my own bed.

# 12

# Family Reunion

Summer drifted on pleasantly, and more simply than term time, because we did not have school. We met our friends for other functions and to enjoy each other's company. The days slipped by quickly.

Then a call came from the United States from Mother and Father. Baby sister was born and doing well. We were told she was a long baby, especially for a girl, was strong, and didn't fuss a lot. Mother was also doing well and already feeling stronger.

This was all good news, but somehow it tugged at our hearts because we knew what it meant leaving this place, which had become a home to us. Our new family had taken us in as one of their own. They had done a good job making us feel at home in Hillbrook. It was a confusing time for Margaret and me.

Henry was not aware of anything at his age, but we felt he also really cared for Aunt Martha and Uncle Harold. He seemed to thrive on the attention they gave him. He probably didn't realize changes were coming.

Mother and Father would be here as soon as Mother was well enough for the long ride. Baby sister would be left with mother's sister, Aunt Janet, who would come to care for baby Ann, our brother and sister, with Mrs. Kessler's help. We would be leaving Aunt and Uncle and going back to our home in Kansas City. I wondered if Henry remembered his little brother and sister, and even knew he had another baby sister.

At times we also worried that Mother and Father may not really want to come to get us. Maybe the family they had at home was enough for them, but they felt they had to come. After all, Margaret said, "If they really loved us, why did they make us come all the way to Canada—so far from our city and friends?"

We wondered if our brother and sister would remember us. Would we be like strangers to them?

We knew that things would change when we arrived home. Margaret would be helping Mother with the younger children. None of us would have as much time to do what we wanted to do, as we did here in Canada.

Father traveled several states in his job, leaving Mother to take care of all of us. We felt sad and asked ourselves, "What can we do"? We were very young to think about these things. We loved our parents, brothers, and sisters and missed being with them, but we had grown used to our life here. Now we were going back and would need to get used to changing our lives again.

I began to worry about all these things, especially about whether Mother and Father really wanted us or if the family was already big enough at home. If that were the case, where would we go? Then I thought of Aunt Martha and Uncle Harold. This change may be hard for them too. Maybe they had gotten used to us and would want us to stay with them.

Finally, Margaret said, "Penelope, you're young. Your thinking is childish." I was only seven, and Margaret was fourteen.

"When we are older and able to think as adults," said Margaret, "we will be able to remember this time we spent in Canada with fond memories." That helped to calm me down a little. I was so glad Margaret was here with me and was able to see things sensibly.

"Mother and Father will be coming soon," she said. "We need to get ourselves ready to say good-bye to Martha and Harold." I knew she wanted to say she would miss Farley too. Saying good-bye to him would be difficult for her, but she didn't say anything else.

The next day when Eileen came to help Aunt Martha at the house, she told us her friend from the military service was coming back home very soon to Hillbrook. He had been wounded in the war and was being discharged from active service. She was so happy he was coming home. Many of their friends in the town had gone to the war, and some had been injured. We had heard some were not coming home, but we didn't mention this to her.

She told us her friend, John, had been wounded in his leg and had spent some months in a hospital recovering. She told us he was walking with a cane and would be home soon. She asked if the family would be able to come to a welcome home party for him on the coming Sunday. She had asked Aunt Martha and Uncle Harold if we would all be able to come. It was to be this Sunday after church. Aunt Martha told Eileen, "We will try."

Since the baby was born, we stopped taking our walks, watching for Mother and Father's Chevrolet. Aunt Martha told us they were starting out in their car on the coming weekend and would be in Hillbrook by Tuesday or Wednesday of the coming week. Aunt Martha said this meant we would all be able to go to Eileen's welcome home party on Sunday for her service friend before our parents arrived.

Margaret and I were happy we would be able to attend the party and meet Eileen's friend, John. We hoped there would be some of our friends there too so we could say good-bye. We wanted to make the best of the time we had left.

We decided to take a last walk around the neighborhood to wave or say good-bye to all of the nice people one more time. We also walked to the new dental office Uncle Harold had just opened. He told us he had more patients and that the office at home was too small now. He was glad to have the room he needed to take better care of his patients.

He said when we all would go home, Eileen agreed to help out in his new dental office. Aunt Martha was to train her to answer the phone and do other dental assistant tasks. Uncle Harold said Eileen was very intelligent, and she had told him she was happy to have the opportunity to learn a new job, especially in his new office.

Everything in the office was new and very shiny. Uncle Harold smiled when he told us about his new office and that Eileen would be a full-time assistant. Margaret and I were happy for Eileen. She always worked hard at Martha and Harold's, and she was very talented.

We walked to the church and the town square where we had enjoyed the fair. Instead of being fun, this only made us feel worse, so we just went home to wait and didn't take any more walks.

On Sunday, we went to church and then to Eileen's parents' house for the welcome home party. We had dressed in our best clothes, and when we arrived at Eileen's house, it was filled with many people. Most of the guests were people I didn't know—friends of the family and their church members.

Eileen had told us that she and John had grown up in the same school, which was also her church. Since John was now a war veteran and had been injured, many of the people were here to thank him for his service and to welcome him home. We didn't know that this was also an engagement party for John and Eileen until Eileen's father announced that they were to be married in the next spring. Their friends clapped and rushed to give them their best wishes.

Margaret and I were so surprised and happy for Eileen. John was smiling and was very handsome. Eileen looked so pretty dressed in a yellow dress with flowers on it. We had never seen Eileen dressed in such pretty clothes. She always wore work clothes with us.

We went up to Eileen and John and told them how happy we were for them both. Then everyone began to get in line for the delicious-looking cake and punch they were serving. As we moved toward the line, I recognized a young woman standing by the cake table. She looked like the woman I had seen in the hotel with Aunt Martha in Saskatoon.

As I moved closer, I saw that she was the same young woman in the restroom who had been crying. In the restroom, when I had asked if she was all right, she had answered, "I'm unable to complete my journey, and I will be staying in Canada for a while. I really don't know for how long."

I had commented on her pretty necklace. It had a ring on it that looked like the ring the other young woman had been wearing in the Union Station train restroom in Kansas

City. Here she was again, talking to the same older man, only today the man was wearing a black suit with a white collar. I went up to them and introduced myself. She said her name was Lisa and called the man "Father."

She said she remembered our conversation, and I told her that my sister and brother and I were going back to the United States where our family lived. I asked if she was able to continue her journey, and she said, "Not at this time."

I reminded her about our meeting, about how I had admired her necklace with a ring and how surprised I was to see it because I had first seen another ring like it on another woman in the train station in Kansas City in the United States.

She looked eagerly at me and grasped my arm. "You saw another ring like mine in America?" she asked. "Can you describe the necklace to me?"

I described the ring to her and told her that the other lady wore her ring on her hand, while she wore hers on a chain under her dress.

"When you took the chain off at the hotel, I saw the ring, which was like hers. You took the ring off of the chain and put it away in your purse. You said it was very special and that you didn't want to lose it."

She looked at me eagerly again with a questioning look on her face and asked if my parents were here. I told her Aunt Martha and Uncle Harold were here with me as well as my brother and sister.

She and her father went with me to meet Aunt Martha and Uncle Harold. After meeting them, they whispered some things and quickly decided to leave the engagement party with us and go to Aunt Martha and Uncle Harold's home.

We all gave best wishes to Eileen and John on their engagement and also to their parents, thanking them for a lovely party. We also thanked John for his service and let him know we were glad he was home and recovering from his injury. We said we wished we could stay longer, but we needed to go.

Margaret and I didn't want to leave because so many young people were there, and we hadn't had any cake and punch. But our family and our two new acquaintances seemed to want to rush out, so we all left. We went back home to Aunt Martha and Uncle Harold's house.

The young woman and her father wanted to talk to me about the other woman at the Union Station, so I told my story again, describing the man who gave the other woman a note and that I thought he was her father.

Then I tried to describe what she looked like. I had to tell them how the women looked a little like each other, except the one at Union Station was a little older and reminded me of my teacher at Woodrow Wilson Grade School.

After I answered all of their questions, they let us all go to get ready for bed. Lisa said, "Thank you, Penny, very much." I didn't know why she thanked me, but I smiled and replied, "You're welcome."

Margaret and I talked about what happened at the party. She told me, "Maybe the two women are related or perhaps went to the same school where everyone received a ring. That is why the rings were alike." She continued, "Anyway, I hope Eileen will still be here helping Aunt Martha next week so we can say good-bye. I will miss her."

I hoped so too.

Time seemed to move slowly for the next couple of days. Then a call came in from Mother and Father. They were in Saskatoon and would be here tomorrow. We were surprised and decided to get our things ready so we didn't leave anything behind we wanted to keep.

I felt sad about leaving Martha and Harold behind. It was so far from our home in Kansas City, and we would not be able to see them very often. They would be sad, and we wouldn't be able to do anything about it.

The next day at lunchtime, Uncle Harold came up to tell us to come downstairs—Mother and Father were here. I was so excited. I dressed in my clothes first and then ran downstairs.

Mother and Father looked almost the same as I remembered. I wanted to hug them but felt shy about it, so I just sat down. Little Henry smiled but stayed on Aunt Martha's lap. Margaret ran to Mother and Father and hugged them.

A little time later, after talking to us, they came over and picked up Henry and me and gave us a hug. Mother, Father as well as Aunt and Uncle did a lot of talking that day. It was a reunion for them as well as us.

We all went to bed early after dinner because the next morning, we were getting up very early for the trip home. When Mother and Father woke us up, it was still dark outside. I was still sleepy and could hardly eat breakfast.

We left quickly after breakfast. Father had loaded the car with our belongings when we were sleeping, so all we had to do after we ate was say good-bye to Aunt Martha and Uncle Harold. They looked very sad but kissed us and told us to be good and to help our mother and father the best we could. Mother and Father were waiting in the car, so we tried to say our good-byes as quickly as possible.

I didn't remember too much about the trip home except we stayed in hotels every night and that the days seemed very long. Mother had never learned to drive, so Father did all of the driving. Mother and Father didn't talk much.

Since Father drove, Mother helped by reading the maps. They didn't talk or smile much. I thought they were probably still tired from the trip to Canada to get us, and now they had to drive another long trip back to our home in America.

We had to stop a lot along the way for all of us to use the restrooms, to eat, and to sleep. The restrooms reminded me of the experiences I had at the train station in Kansas

City and the hotel in Saskatoon. I thought about the two young women who wore pretty rings that were alike.

This made me feel tired. I slept a lot dreaming about the women and asking myself who they were and why they looked a little like each other but spoke differently. Where did they come from, and why were they wearing rings that were alike?

Sleeping helped the time to pass, and soon we crossed over into the United States and were on our way home. I was beginning to feel excited, wanting time to pass more quickly that it would not be so long before I would see my brother and sister again. I hoped they would remember me. My new baby sister wouldn't know me, but if I played with her a lot, she would learn.

We ate at a restaurant where Father went in and got the food. We continued to drive while we ate in the car. We had hamburgers and milk shakes. I had never had a hamburger at a restaurant before. It was the best hamburger I had ever eaten, even though Mother cooked good hamburgers.

Margaret was helping Mother to keep track of the miles on the map, and she would tell us when we were in Minnesota and then Iowa and then Missouri. We went through so many towns I couldn't name them.

When we reached Missouri, my heart started to pound in my chest. I was close to home, and my heart was telling me it won't be long now. The sun went down, and darkness was closing in when we finally reached our home.

Mother's sister, Janet, had been called and was looking out the window for our car. We saw her after passing our house. We turned the corner to the alley and parked in the back next to where the garage was located.

We all got out, and each of us carried something into the house to help Father. Mother looked more tired than Father but helped with as much of our belongings as she could. Everything in the yard and the house looked the same as I remembered.

When we were all inside, Auntie Janet hugged us and helped Mother to a seat on the couch in the living room. "I'm glad you're finally home," she said and sat down next to Mother.

My little brother, Albert, and my sister, Katherine, were looking at us like they knew us but weren't sure what to do. They had grown taller and bigger all over, and their curly hair was a little darker. They were very cute, and when I smiled and said hello to each of them saying their names, I think that was when they remembered me. I pulled out from behind my back two small packages.

"I have presents for you," I said. "They're books from Canada. When you go to bed, I'll come up and read them to you."

Albert and Katherine looked at each other and said words I didn't understand.

"They're talking a lot," Mother said. "Sometimes I don't know what they are talking about, but I think they know what each other is saying."

Baby sister, Ann, was asleep in bed, so only Mother and Father could get close to see her. The rest of us looked from the doorway. "She is so little and cute," Margaret said.

I wanted to hold her but knew that I would have to wait. Mother would have me sit down first and then place her in my arms like she did with Henry, Katherine, and Albert after they were born. I was happy to be home, but with so much going on, I hoped I wouldn't forget Aunt Martha and Uncle Harold. I started to think about them and wondered what they were doing tonight. I didn't know why, but I missed them. I was home where I wanted to be, but I did miss Aunt Martha and Uncle Harold and wished they lived in our town or that we lived closer.

The events of the past months and now our being home again with all my mixed feelings seemed a mystery to me. As I lay in bed that night in my old familiar room, it seemed to me that life was full of mysteries that I didn't know how to solve.

# 13

# A New Start

Mother was anxious that we all get back into our schedules, as she called them. The new school term was beginning soon.

Margaret was transferred into her first year of high school. Henry started kindergarten, and I graduated to the second grade. I was surprised I was promoted to the second grade and was sure they would realize their mistake, but I didn't say anything about it. I thought that the grading might be different in Canada.

Mother was a little worried that Margaret and I would be behind in school, but I didn't know why she thought we would have trouble in our new grades. In Canada, our grade cards were good enough, and we were passed on.

I did remember my teacher kept telling me to work and to try harder. I didn't know if that meant I wasn't really doing well or that if I worked harder, I could do better.

Either way, it didn't take too long for me to know what to do at Woodrow Wilson School since I had already attended there.

I recognized some of my friends in school, but some I didn't remember. There were more students in my class this year than last year and a lot more than at Hillbrook. Henry and I walked to school together in the morning, but Mother had to come for him at noon since he was only in school for half a day. In a few weeks, however, the school called Mother to come for a meeting.

They told her Henry was ready for first grade and that they could advance him but only with Mother and Father's permission. So they decided Henry was to start the first grade and skip kindergarten the following Monday. After this was settled, Henry and I began walking to and from school together every day.

Mother seemed much stronger than she was before we had left for Canada. Mrs. Kessler helped her, and since Father was still traveling a lot, it was good that she was with us to help Mother.

One day when I came home from school, Mother told us she had a telephone call to invite the family to a friend's church. There was to be a dinner, and it was to be on a Sunday afternoon, a couple of weeks from now. Mother seemed to worry a little about this and told us we would be going shopping for new clothes.

The following Saturday, Father and Mother decided to take Margaret and me "downtown" for new clothes. Our little brother and sisters were too young and wouldn't be coming with us to the friend's church. Mrs. Kessler agreed to stay with them.

Mrs. Kessler was an interesting person. Sunday was her day off, and she always went to her own church and to dinner every Sunday. She had been born in Germany but came to America with her parents some years ago.

She didn't say how many years it had been, but I thought it was a good time to come to America because they had a relative here and thought it better to move when a relative was here in America to help them.

Mother and Father didn't seem to mind her being German despite the war, and when they asked her, she told them she was an American. She must have been lonely, though, when she moved here with us. She said her husband had died and that now her church friends were all she had left.

Her church denomination was called Lutheran. When I asked her about her church, she told Margaret and me about the man who founded it. His name was Martin Luther. "He was a brave man and lived a long time ago," she said.

Margaret and I liked Mrs. Kessler. She treated us like we were members of her family. Mother was very happy she had agreed to help her by taking care of Ann, Katherine, Albert, and Henry when we went to the church dinner. Mother told her how much she appreciated her giving up her Sunday to help the family. She told her to pick any other day off during the week, or even a Saturday, if she wanted a weekend off. Mrs. Kessler said she couldn't think of any time she would need but would keep it in mind, especially if the church had needs during the holidays.

Father didn't like to shop, but Mother said he had to go because he also needed a new suit. Father hadn't bought himself clothes since before the war had started, and he knew Mother was right. Mrs. Kessler took care of baby sister Ann, little brother Albert, Henry, and younger sister Katherine, and the rest of us went shopping.

It became a very long and tiring day. When we were all ready to come home, I thought we had all we needed. It turned out to be a lucky day because Mother and Father picked a very pretty dress for me—the prettiest dress I ever had with a bow to tie around the waist.

I also got patent leather shoes. Margaret got a pretty more grown-up dress since she was now a high school girl. Father got his new suit, which he said was a good idea. Mother said she didn't need a new dress because "I have clothes, and at last, I'm able to fit into them."

So now all we had to do was to wait to wear our new clothes. I began thinking why was it you had to wait for the good things to happen? This year, we had done a lot of waiting. I decided I should learn how to wait since I was not good at it.

Then I started to wonder why we were going to this new church. When I asked Mother, she said, "It's nothing to worry about. It's a surprise! It'll be here before you know it, and you will just have to wait."

# 14

# A Surprise

Finally, the Sunday came we were going to the new church for dinner. After a lot of activity getting ourselves ready to go, we hurried to the first service at our church. I tried to keep my new dress from wrinkling, but I couldn't help getting some wrinkles.

After church we got back into the car the second time to go to the new church for dinner. My bow got crumpled again, so I gave up trying to keep my dress nice. I thought about what the new church would be like and what we would have for dinner. I also wondered who had invited us and why Mother had said that it was a surprise.

When Father said, "Well, we're here," I looked up and had to climb up and over Margaret to see. It was a big beautiful church. It was mostly made of stones with lots of colored glass windows.

There was a large parking lot, but Father didn't know where he should park or where the front door was until we saw some people parking and going in. Father parked as close as we could so we could go into the door the other people had entered.

When we walked in, there were people waiting. I thought they were waiting for us because as we entered, they came rushing to us. "Come in and welcome!" They all smiled and exclaimed. A smaller group stood nearby, and my heart began to beat very hard when I looked at them.

Two young women in the group, together with the others, looked familiar and were smiling at us. At first, I thought I was having a dream, and I couldn't think. They looked like the two young women I had met in the train station and the hotel in Saskatoon.

They called out, "Penny!" and rushed toward me. They held my hands and said, "We're here together—you brought us together." Margaret looked surprised, and her mouth hung open.

Mother and Father smiled and said, "This party is for you, Penny, and for these two young women who wanted to thank you for bringing them together." I looked at them and started to cry. I remembered all the times I had wondered about them and all the questions I had asked myself about who they could be.

I remembered the young woman in Saskatoon who was lost and so sad. I remembered how I had met her in the hotel restroom and how she had said she didn't know where she was going. I remembered the other older lady in our train station that was also new to America and had to say good-bye to whom I thought was her father. She had acted a little afraid about being in our country.

They both had dark hair and were alike somehow in their looks. They both had similar rings too, but their languages were different. It was a mystery that had filled my thoughts. I stopped crying when I looked at them and realized they were here together and were smiling.

Wiping the tears away from my face, I began to ask them questions: who were they? Why were we all here?

"Let's have dinner, and we can talk about ourselves and when and how we met," the younger woman, Lisa, said.

That was a good idea because I had many questions, and the church ladies had the dinner ready and had already begun to serve everyone. It smelled delicious. I wanted to hear more from the two women but realized we would have to wait.

We all sat down at the tables set for us. The church ladies set our dinners down in front of us when we were seated. Then another father said a prayer of thanksgiving for our food and many blessings.

Even though dinner looked and smelled delicious, I wasn't able to eat much with my mind so anxious to hear the stories of these two young women. The church members were asking if we needed anything—more water, tea—but

I was more interested in learning about the young women, who they were, and where they came from.

I just wanted to hear about their lives and to learn some answers to my questions. I didn't eat very much and hoped dinner would be over soon. When dessert was served, the two young women got up and moved to the front of the room to begin to tell their stories. The oldest, Lauren, spoke first. She stood up and began speaking.

"After graduating from the convent school in Paris where our Mother was a teacher, I began working at an engineering firm upon completion of their training program. It was an intern position, learning various office skills. My uncle, an engineer and a former employee of this firm, referred me and helped me to find this position. I wanted to go to a university, but with the prospect of war, I put future plans on hold. I am seven years older than my sister, Lisa, and lived with her in an apartment with our mother and father.

Early in the war in France, Paris was beginning to be occupied by the Nazis. Our father joined the French underground to work with the resistance. Our mother continued her teaching at the convent school while I continued working in my new position."

With relief, I understood that this answered my main question: who were they? They were sisters, and Lauren was the oldest!

"As the occupation of Paris continued, our mother became worried for Lisa and made an arrangement with her fellow teacher friend, Kathleen, to travel with her youngest daughter to England and possibly on to Ireland. Kathleen had decided early in the war to try to return to Ireland, her homeland. Our mother asked Kathleen if she could take Lisa with her until it was safe for Lisa to return. Kathleen agreed. She promised to take care of her, as if she were her own sister or daughter. After the appropriate paperwork was signed and arrangements were made, Lisa would leave with Kathleen. Their plan was to immigrate to the British Isles and eventually to Ireland where Kathleen had been born. They were going to cross the channel by ship as soon as arrangements were made. Timeliness was very important because we had heard the Nazis were invading Belgium and the Netherlands. Also more frightening, more uniformed Nazi officers were appearing frequently in and around Paris."

Lauren continued to relate their story. "After Lisa and Kathleen left on their journey, I continued working at my new job and living in the apartment with my mother, who was still teaching at the convent school. Knowledge of Father's whereabouts became scant. Eventually, we began to fear he was never coming home. One day after returning home from my work, I found Mother was not yet home from her teaching job at the convent. Concerned, I went to the school to check on a possible reason for her delay. The teachers who were still at the school told me some Nazi officers came to the school looking for her. They told the school it was just a routine check and that they needed to ask her some questions. Another teacher said she saw them take Mother away by automobile.

"When she didn't return after a couple days, I became very worried, especially since Father was in the Resistance. I decided to go to my father and mother's good friends, Louie and Marie, for advice. They owned a bakery and had been friends for as many years as I could remember. They told me to pack all of my personal items and leave our apartment, telling the apartment manager I was moving out of Paris for a new job. They said to give notice at my place of work and to tell the few friends I had left an identical story. I moved in with Louie and Marie, whose business was baking bread and other bakery items for the neighborhood. They were a couple, a little older than my parents, with no children of their own. They lived in an apartment above the bakery, which was small but had an extra spare room I could use as a bedroom.

"They said I should keep a very low profile. If their older customers inquired about who I was, they would tell them I was a niece who came to Paris looking for a job. Most of the bakery work was done in the early hours of each day. They said I could help with the work, but only if I wanted to help. I was overwhelmed by their kindness to me, and I did try to learn baking and to help them in any way I was able. I especially stayed close to the bakery and, through the years before the war was over, did what I could to maintain the image they had established for me.

"They were a religious couple who attended church regularly. They were known by all of the neighbors. The neighbors often helped them when the need arose, which became more frequent as the war progressed. Eventually, I realized, except for their kindness and friendship, that I was alone. I continued to live in the bakery. Future plans for my life were put in the back of my mind. Survival was always foremost on my mind. Eventually, I thought when the war is over, I might be able to make plans and try to reunite with my remaining family. I had kept some of the letters from my mother's sister, Jeanne, and her husband, Benjamin, when they immigrated to America before the war had begun to escalate. They were fortunate the United States accepted their emigration applications in the late thirties. Jeanne and Benjamin had heard frightening stories about some of their friends and public officials in France disappearing.

Jeanne's husband was an engineer who had graduated from an engineering school in Belgium and was also Jewish. They had decided to immigrate to the United States while they were still able to leave France and the United States was not involved in the war."

Lauren went on to explain. "When Kathleen and Lisa arrived in England, they quickly went on to Kathleen's home in Ireland. When they arrived in Dublin, they wrote letters to Lisa's home in Paris. But unfortunately, our mother never received any letters regarding these plans. I had mailed letters to Kathleen and Lisa but never received a response from either of them. Letters stopped coming, and occasionally, some of our long-time friends just disappeared. As time went on, the occupation increased. After several months, the American and Allied troops arrived on French soil with more war and battles continuing.

"Finally, the war was over. Jubilation was everywhere. In my grieving heart, I began to feel relief and hope. Because of Louie and Marie, I had survived. I began to hope that God willing, I might begin the search to find my remaining family. However, how would I ever be able to thank Louie and Marie? I had learned to care deeply for them. Their welfare was upmost in my mind, and yet when I talked about trying to find my sister and Aunt and Uncle, they unhesitatingly said, 'God would never have allowed us such good fortune, living through this terrible war and such devastation, if it was not his will. You must find your family. We believe you will. Do what you can and don't give up hope.'

"The country was beginning to show signs of recovery with the Allied countries aiding us. It was then I began to plan. Where should I begin? I wanted to find my sister in England or in Ireland and my family in America. I had heard that Great Britain experienced repeated bombing raids in villages, farms, and schools. I told myself if I had family left in America, they might be able to help me find Lisa. I was hopeful and began communicating with an agency called the International Refugee Agency and with churches and individuals in Canada affiliated with our church. I corresponded with and eventually became acquainted with Father Francis, hoping he might help me find my aunt and uncle and my dear sister, Lisa.

"After much communication and support of many people, I was able to come to the United States. As many of you know, I found my aunt and uncle and am living with them in Kansas City. They have been an amazing support for me. I am teaching French and working in the administrative office of a small private school. I feel God has been with us and has blessed us more than we were able to imagine. My next plan was to look for Lisa. This is only part of mine and Lisa's story. I am so happy to introduce my sister, Lisa, to share the rest of our story with you."

At this time, the guests attending this dinner stood up on their feet, applauding and cheering. I stood up with everyone and cheered with them. Hearing Lauren's story answered many questions I had, but there were more answers to come.

The younger sister, Lisa, rose from her chair in the front of the room where she was sitting. When she reached Lauren, she looked at her, and tears began to cover her eyes and face. They embraced, and Lauren took Lisa's hands and, holding them, said, "We're together now. Please tell your story, Lisa, so everyone will understand how grateful we are that we found each other and that we are in the United States of America."

# 15

## Answers

Lisa began her story. "I was very young, eleven years old and still attending the convent school when I left with Kathleen for England and then Ireland. Mother was very worried about the events going on in Paris and in Europe. She felt I would be safer living in England. Mother prepared the appropriate paperwork for my education to continue on schedule. She included my medical records and her written permission for Kathleen to assume responsibility for me, giving her permission to make decisions on my behalf. We all felt Mother had done all she was able to do to set me on a good course. But of course, no one can know all the changes that can occur, especially in the difficult, complicated times in which we were all living.

"Kathleen and I left on our journey out of France and to England on a ship. It wasn't a passenger ship in the true sense but more like a cargo ship delivering goods to England, France, and back. It was a busy ship. The captain and the working men kept the ship moving, we hoped, toward England. Initially, Kathleen and I got seasick. The ocean waters were rough, and the ship was tossed about with the stormy weather conditions. Gradually, the sea became calmer, and our seasickness subsided. We spent most of our time in our sleeping compartments thinking it best to stay out of the seamen's way. The men were very busy maintaining the ship with the unpredictable stormy weather conditions and with the direction the ship was traveling.

"Eventually, we arrived at a small dock on the coastline of England. An uncle of Kathleen's named Gerald was there to greet us and take us to our next destination. He was an older gentleman, and he tried to assist us in any way possible. He was very friendly, but the problem was he had a way of talking that I didn't understand and, of course, I only spoke French. It was a good thing Kathleen could speak both languages. Gerald had a horse and buggy. He said he would take us to the first destination, but we would need to hurry. The Blitzkrieg, which Gerald explained to us, was an airplane bomb attack, and he added we would be required to go to a shelter if the siren sounded. So we quickly got into the buggy to continue our journey.

"We didn't stop until we ended up at his family farm house a few hours from where our travel ship had docked. Gerald told us we would stay the night. The following morning, we would continue our journey to Ireland with his son, William. He told us we would probably be safer in Ireland, especially if there was bombing in England. We later learned William was a young man who was unable to join the Royal Navy like many of his former school friends had. The family never explained to us the reason why he wasn't serving, but later we learned he had developed a heart problem in his youth, which made him ineligible for military service.

"William was very pleasant-looking, tall, and thin with a very friendly smile. He agreed to assist us with our journey. Gerald and his wife, Gladys, William's parents, were very kind to us. She had dinner ready, along with a nice warm bed for us to sleep in. We were very tired, but before dinner, we said a grace. We thought we heard sirens and possibly planes and explosions. Later Kathleen and I said a prayer for all those experiencing a Blitzkrieg. Kathleen was very happy we were on our way the next morning to her home and seemed to be in good spirits, especially after such a cozy rest. We thanked Gerald and Gladys for their hospitality and watched as they resumed their morning chores when we left with William.

"Their farm was a very quiet, even lonely-looking, place with no neighbors close by, but they had a beautiful view of the ocean, a lot of work in their garden to keep up, and livestock to attend to. We decided they probably loved their farm and didn't think it was lonely there at all.

That morning, we were moving quickly after a good rest. William drove the horse faster than his father, but it still took the day and into the evening for us to reach the next phase of our journey. Kathleen and William began to do a lot of talking as the day went on. They talked about some friends they both knew, even though William was younger and didn't live in Kathleen's city. Eventually, lights from another town came into view, and William said we would rest here at least for the night.

"The rest of the trip took a few days with each visit adding a different driver. We traveled early in the day and on roads that were not well traveled. I thought the drivers talked about riding northward toward Liverpool. I learned we would then cross a channel there. We would cross the channel on a ferry leaving England and going to Ireland. Even though I was not sure of our location throughout the trip, I felt confident the drivers knew where we were and where we were going. Throughout our journey, we saw many soldiers. Some looked very young. Kathleen and I talked about these brave young men and wished we could thank them for their service. Prayers were all we could give them. We thought that maybe we would be able to volunteer our time in some way to express our appreciation.

"When we finally arrived in Dublin, Kathleen was overjoyed to be reunited with her family. Her mother and father welcomed us and me as if I was a member of their family. With the family helping us, we seemed to settle in quickly. Bedtime and sleep beckoned to us, and we succumbed gratefully. Kathleen's mother took charge of my enrollment in school to help me get started quickly. It was very much like the convent school I had attended in Paris. The family took good care of me, and slowly I began to learn their Irish language. Soon I took part in the family routine. With Kathleen's help, I wrote letters to all my travel friends, especially William, thanking them for all of their kindnesses.

"I prayed to see my family again but kept busy doing anything I could to help Kathleen's family. I cooked some meals for them, which they praised me for, even though I knew they weren't perfect. Some of the food I cooked was different from theirs, so I learned their type of cooking as well. We all prayed for the war to be over. I helped with the work as if I were home and tried to not add to their worries. The months went by quickly, and I continued with my schooling the best I was able, even though after the eighth grade at the convent school, there was no school for me to attend. Most of the convent students stopped going to school and began working when they completed the eighth grade.

"Some students attended the private schools called 'public schools' that required fees. Other older students with scholarships went on to the universities. Since I had no resources, I expected to try to find work after the eighth grade. Kathleen's family had fun together. They were very musical, and in the beginning years with them, they began to teach me to play the piano and the fiddle. After a time and to my amazement, I performed with them and their friends in the local establishments in the area. They were very supportive of my interests in music. Surprisingly, I learned quickly and also sang some.

"I was with Kathleen's family for almost six years. My family in Paris seemed almost like a dream when the war was over. Thoughts of joining my family started to become a reality I wanted. But I really loved my new adopted family so much, and I didn't know what I should do. I wasn't sure I wanted to leave. By the end of the war, Paris had been devastated. Because I had not heard from my family in Paris and I had other family who had immigrated to the United States, I decided to begin the search there. Our Irish friends thought a passageway through Canada might be a good place to start.

"My Irish family encouraged me to move forward with a positive attitude. Kathleen's father told me I must look for my family in America. He said, 'We love you, Lisa, and if you decide you want to come back to live with us, we will welcome you, but you must try to find your family in America first. Always remember, it is your decision to choose where home is.' This gave me the confidence to start my search.

"Eventually, with the help of church friends, I entered Canada and ended up in the middle of the country in the province of Saskatchewan. I was sponsored by a couple helping war-torn emigrants looking for family in the United States. I vaguely remembered Aunt Jeanne and her husband Ben's letters indicating the beautiful farms and county side in the middle of the country, so we were starting our search in the Midwest of the United States. Our church was doing some work for me as well. Around this time, I had met and found friendships in my church.

"I was invited to a wedding announcement party for a couple and would be attending it with friends. They told me it would be good for me to go to a party for a change, so I said yes. As it turned out, it was a long drive there, and I hoped I wouldn't regret my decision. It was at this party that I saw Penny. I remembered her and our conversation at the hotel in Saskatoon when we had first spoken. After speaking with her again, my friends and I left with her family to their home in Hillbrook. Penny, with her brother and sister, were in Hillbrook from the United States visiting their aunt and uncle. This conversation opened up my world! It was the beginning of the end of my search."

At this moment in Lisa's story, I started to tremble with excitement, and tears began to stream down my face. I was shaken when both sisters said, "Penny, please come up to us."

I felt I could hardly walk. My legs were so weak, but somehow I moved up to the front with the sisters. Looking at me, they said, "Thank you, Penny, for bringing us together. Because you recognized something familiar in us and with a little nudging from the Lord, we have found each other." They each took a hand, smiled, and hugged me. "We'll never be able to thank you enough!"

My eyes filled with tears of joy and amazement. Shaken, I stared at the sisters smiling at me. I remembered my mother saying, "When someone thanks you, you should always say, 'You're welcome.'" Since I couldn't think of anything else to say, I said, "You're welcome."

# 16

## A Wish Fulfilled

I looked around at all of the church members and friends hovering around Lauren and Lisa. I looked back at Mother, Father, and Margaret sitting at our table. They were smiling and beckoning to me to join them. I realized there would be school tomorrow and that Father may need to travel with his work. Maybe that is why they want me to come and sit down with them—so they can tell me that we need to be leaving.

"Do we need to leave soon?" I asked them as I sat down.

"In a few minutes," Father said.

Just then, Lauren and Lisa walked toward us, joining us at our table.

Lauren spoke first. "Penny, Lisa and I have something to tell you and to ask you. We are so grateful to you that you helped bring us together. We are the last of our remaining family each of us has. We want to do something for you to show our appreciation, and so you know how grateful we are and how happy you helped us to be. We've already spoken to your parents, and your mother has suggested something to us. She told us you had asked to take piano lessons like your sister, Margaret. She said your family has a piano in the entry hall."

Lisa spoke up next and said, "Penny, I am a piano teacher, and giving you piano lessons would be a small way I could show my appreciation to you, to thank you for bringing Lauren and me together. I could come to your home after school once a week for lessons. I teach piano and violin at the same school Lauren works. Also, here's some more for you to think about. The next year when you would be starting the third grade, we would like to know if you would be able to visit our school at an open house. You and your family could come for a visit. It is a school only girls attend. If you and your parents agree, Lauren and I would like to sponsor you at our school. You would be able to meet girls from all over the city, and some of the girls are even from different countries. The school starts with kindergarten and goes through the eighth grade. You would come and go home from school on a school bus. The bus would pick you up at your home.

"If you like the school and if your parents agree, then Katherine and Ann could attend when they are ready for kindergarten. Albert would start at Woodrow Wilson when he is ready, and he and Henry would go to school together. Since Margaret is in high school now, she would continue there."

My heart leapt, and I smiled at Lisa and looked at my parents. Mother looked at me and said, "Father and I agreed to the piano lessons but only if you want them and would practice. We can talk about you starting a new school next fall, Penny. We can visit the school, and we have time to make that decision. This is a lot of change, Penny, so you have a lot to think about."

I looked around at everyone and then thought for a few moments and then replied, "I have always wanted to learn to play the piano. Margaret still plays the piano, and she helps the teachers at our Sunday school by playing. Yes, I would love to have lessons, and I will practice every day!"

Lisa said, "That's wonderful, Penny. We will be able to start your lessons when your mother says you are ready. This also means we will be able to see you often, which will be a great pleasure for us!"

I looked at my new friends and said, "Thank you very much," and went to them to hug them. Then Mother and Father stood up, and they all smiled while everyone shook hands and hugged each other.

Father said his thank-you to Lisa and Lauren for the fine dinner. Mother added she would call soon to invite them to our home for dinner. "If you think you both would be able to handle dinner with six children," she added laughingly as she said it.

Lauren and Lisa said they would love to come to dinner and that six children are not so many. Lauren said, "We see many more children at the school where we teach every day. In fact, when the school finishes for the year and summer comes, the school has an open house, and the older girls in the school taking music lessons give a recital. We'll call you about the date. If you are able, we would love to have you all come."

We all said we would look forward to going to the recital. "Thank you again," Mother said. "I'll call soon about the lessons and dinner."

On the way home, Margaret said, "This will be fun with you playing the piano. After lessons for six years, I still remember just about everything. Eventually, we may be able to play duets."

I heard Margaret's words, but other thoughts took over. I wondered what the school would be like if all of the students were just girls. "I don't think they would pick kickball to play at recess," I thought out loud. "I might like to go to a school where all the students are girls and some of them from other countries." Margaret just looked at me and stopped talking.

Then I thought about how lucky everyone at the church was tonight. The sisters had found each other. Henry, Margaret, and I were home with our family. Mother didn't have dark circles around her eyes anymore. She had Mrs. Kessler to help her, and she could wear her regular clothes again finally. Father didn't seem to be as worried. At least, he seemed to enjoy being at home and smiled more.

Maybe some of these good things happened because the war was over, I thought. However, not everyone we knew was as happy as we were tonight. Some had problems left to solve, while some family members were still missing and not coming home.

It was then I thought about war. I decided war is a bad thing. I couldn't think of anything good about it or why we had to have wars. Why couldn't people talk about their problems to solve them?

Margaret and I talked about our problems. We told each other our ideas. We thought about the others' ideas, and sometimes their ideas seemed better. If we didn't like others' ideas better, at least, we heard each other and tried to understand their thinking.

I decided this was too difficult for me to solve because people didn't like it when others didn't agree with them, or they looked different, or even go to a different church. What do we do then? Are these differences as important as what I learned in church school when I was a small child? We should care for and about others as much as we care for and about ourselves.

I felt it was a good time to say my prayers and thank God for all our blessings and for all we had to look forward to— the dinner with the sisters, the piano lessons, and maybe a new school. But as usual, I reflected, "We have to wait for it all to happen."

Then I thought about Aunt Martha and Uncle Harold. Every once in a while, I thought about what they were doing this evening. I hoped Harold's new dental office was big enough and working out for him. Aunt Martha and Eileen would be helping him in the office. Eileen would be a helpful person. She liked people. I missed seeing them.

*I'm going to write a letter tomorrow. Margaret will help me write another letter again. I have a lot of news to tell them.*

# 17

## Pictures

Father and Mother at home in Kansas City, Missouri

Margaret, Henry and Penny, the summer before
Penny began kindergarten in Kansas City

Uncle Harold and Aunt Martha, home in Canada

Bessborough Hotel opened in 1935 in
Saskatoon, Saskatchewan, Canada

Aunt Martha and Uncle Harold's home in Hillbrook

Photograph of a painting of the Hillbrook School

Hillbrook Church

Loon Lake in Saskatchewan, Canada

Henry and Penny prior to leaving Canada
to return to Kansas City

CPSIA information can be obtained
at www.ICGtesting.com
Printed in the USA
FSOW03n0420190517
34182FS